Delta Days:

Tales From the

Mississippi Delta

Thomas R. Lawrence

A Schiel & Denver Softcover

Delta Days: Tales From The Mississippi Delta

First published in 2011 by Schiel & Denver Publishing Limited

10685-B Hazelhurst Drive Suite 8575

Houston, Texas USA 77043

www.schieldenver.com

ISBN 978-1-84903-078-6

Printed in the United States of America and United Kingdom.

Typeset by Schiel & Denver Publishing Limited.

All papers used by Schiel & Denver Publishing are natural recyclable products made from wood grown in well-managed forests. The manufacturing processes conform to the environmental regulations of the country of origin.

Acknowledgements

I have been graced with help and assistance throughout the writing and publishing of this book. Mary Rainer Belford, my administrative assistant as well as my daughter, has provided editorial advice, proof-reading and critical review. Additionally, Mary, who is an accomplished graphic designer, provided the illustrations that accompany the title page to each of my stories.

My good friend and regionally-acclaimed artist, Deborah Fagan Carpenter, generously provided one of her original oil paintings from her series on the Mississippi Delta as the background for the book's cover. She also was kind enough to read through the first draft of the manuscript and offer suggestions that I believe strengthened the book.

My lifelong friend, Lisa Williams Davis, who apparently paid close attention in Miss Brelands English classes, kindly read, proofed and corrected the final manuscript. I am a lost ball in high weeds when it comes to grammar and punctuation. There is universal agreement on this.

I reached back to junior high school and asked my Cleveland classmate, Carolyn Buckles Armstrong to read the manuscript and write a pre-publication review of the book. She graciously did so.

I particularly want to thank my wife, Elaine, for her patience and forbearance. She has been a constant support during this effort and has managed to keep her sense of humor in the process.

I would be remiss if I didn't acknowledge the un-flappable professionalism of my contact at Schiel & Denver. Jacob Peters patiently led this total neophyte through the writing, editing and publishing process while never losing his cool. I choked on several occasions, Jacob never did. Schiel & Denver did everything they promised, did it on time and within our budget. I can recommend them without reservation.

I believe it is very important for those of us who would be writers to express our appreciation to the many Independent Book Sellers that provide the major markets for our books. Owning and managing an independent bookstore has got to be a labor of love. I believe these wonderfully colorful and interesting people are important to our culture and need and deserve our continued support. God Bless 'em everyone!

Dedication

I wrote these stories for several reasons. I have long wanted to chronicle what it was like growing up in the Mississippi Delta, in the 1940s and 50s, a special time and place. I witnessed the last vestige of the plantation mentality on a day to day basis, and in the face of political correctness; I have to admit that I understood both the good and the bad of the era. I want my grandchildren to have some first-hand idea of my childhood, and this book is dedicated first to them, Jackson, Virginia, Ava and Abby.

The second reason I wrote this is to touch again the long standing friendships of my youth. Writing these stories allowed me to relive some of the happiest moments of my life. Many of these friends are still around, many still living in the Delta; these stories are dedicated to these wonderful guys and girls that made the Delta such an interesting place, y'all know who you are. It is also dedicated to those who have passed away in the last fifty years:

Elizabeth Stansel

Tom and Kate Bernhardt

Otho and Kate Rainer

Mary Rose Story

Mr. & Mrs. Edward Story

Edward Story

Ike Turner

Joseph and Kathleen Lawrence

Emmet "Bubba" Rose

Raymond Hazzard

M/Sgt Ike Galtelli

Lt. Col. James H. Milstead

Bobby Farrar

Father Emmon Mullen

Katherine Ward

John Wong

Coach Margaret Wade

Coach "Wig" Reily

Kristen Merritt

Catherine Jones

Effie Glasscoe

Percy & Virginia Funchess

Lucy Douglas

W.J. Parks

If I have left anyone out, it was not intentionally, but the product of a seventy-year-old memory.

The final and most important reason that I finally wrote these stories, is that I had to do it. I can thank my mother, Kathleen Lloyd Lawrence, for the desire to write, and for whatever ability I have to do it. She never got a chance to write her stories, and that's a shame.

Table Of Contents

A Christmas Tale

I was playing on the front platform of the ice and coal company my grandfather owned in Cumberland, Mississippi. The wind swirled down from a gray sky of scudding dark clouds and eddied around the building with tiny bits of snow and sleet. My grandmother had me bundled right up to the point of immobility; I could barely move, but I was toasty warm.

The ice business fell off dramatically in the winter months, but the sale of coal made up for any loss of income. The drivers were returning from their delivery routes and waited to go into my grandfather's office to check-out for the day. I knew them all, and they doted on me like a young prince. This was my favorite time of day.

I'd walked over to the group of laughing black men and said, "Hi y'all, how'd it go today?"

"It went fine, Mr. Tommy, but it looks like it may get cold tonight," responded Louis.

Louis was a light-colored Negro about 45 years old. He was wearing faded blue jeans, a flannel shirt, rumpled work jacket and an old flannel hat with earflaps. His hands were large and calloused, the hands of a working man. Louis, along with Wade, Tracy and John were pretty close to the top of the social and economic order in the local Negro community. They were wage earners and not field hands. They were a little less than the preachers and teachers, but not sharecroppers and they were my friends.

"Well, Mr. Tommy, you all excited about it being Christmas Eve?" Wade asked with a huge grin on his coal black face.

"I really am. I was only four last year at Christmas, and I don't remember much about it, but now that I am five, I can't wait."

"What's Santa Claus gonna bring you?" Tracy chimed in.

"Santa Claus has got me a little worried. Benny's big brother, Ron, told us today that there wasn't any real Santa Claus. Besides, we don't have a chimney."

The plant foreman, a one-legged older Negro called Crip, came up.

"Don't you worry none Mr. Tommy, Ron Story would sit on the stump and swear the tree's never been there. He probably don't know the truth when he sees it. I plan to stay up and let Santa down my ladder when he lands on the roof. He'll get in."

Crip had been working at the plant since my grandfather purchased it in the early 1930's. A former railroad employee, Crip had lost his leg during an accident and was let go, as a result. Grandfather hired him and helped him learn to use a crutch. They were good friends, within the frame work of race relations in Mississippi during the 1940's.

Not only was it Christmas Eve, but it was Saturday and pay day. As soon as everybody got checked out and accounted for the route cash, my grandfather would pay them their weekly wages. Today they would also get their Christmas bonus. Excitement was in the air.

By the time everyone had checked out and picked up their pay and bonus, it was close to 4:00, and Crip told them all to go home early. With a round of Merry Christmas!, the guys left to go buy presents for their children. Crip and I were sitting on one of the wooden benches used by the platform workers and watching the afternoon turn to an early winter night. The snow began to come down in great fluffy flakes and was sticking to the grass in Mrs. Denson's yard across our gravel parking lot.

"Looks like we gonna have a white Christmas this year, just like Mr. Crosby's new song." Crip mused.

"I like that song; it's my favorite Christmas song." I said.

"Yep, it's mighty pretty."

"Crip, what are you gonna do tonight?"

"I'll go over to my son's house. We'll eat dinner and have our Christmas."

"I didn't know Negroes had Christmas."

"Why we sure do, just like you white folks. We open presents in the morning and go to Church."

"I'm glad you are going to have Christmas. I was kinda worried about you and the boys."

"Don't you fret, Mr. Tommy, yo' granpa gave everybody a nice bonus, we'll do just fine. Let's go shut the big momma down and send everybody home."

The "big momma" was the twenty foot-high Fairbanks Morse diesel engine that powered the entire plant. It sat just outside the kitchen door to our apartment, and its constant thumpa-thumpa-thumpa was the background for life in the ice plant. I loved the big momma. I loved the way it smelled: a combination of diesel fumes, machine oil, and high quality leather. I loved the thumpa-thumpa-thumpa, and the feel of the vibrations that pulsed through the concrete foundation. I loved to watch the workmen shut it down every evening, and start it back up every morning. Crip made sure I was always on hand for these daily rites.

The procedure to shut big momma down required two major operations. First, it was necessary to make sure that any secondary systems that could not be shut down were connected to their auxiliary power sources. Crip and I took care of that. We made an inspection tour along the entire 150 foot length of spinning shaft that big momma powered. The belts driving the artesian well were put in neutral, until the plant cranked back up on the day after Christmas. All was ready for the shut down.

Crip turned the fuel valve to off and the thumpa- thumpa began to slow down and finally was stilled. Big momma was ready for Christmas. With the big momma shut down, the deck of ice cans would begin to thaw. That was alright. We had a week or more supply of ice in the cold storage and demand was at its winter's low. Any time you left the engine room; there was a hint of ammonia throughout the plant. Ammonia was a key component of the ice-making process, and we were never without its pungent reminder.

Crip and the rest of the employees left for home, and I went into the kitchen from the engine room. My grandmother was busy preparing supper, and I climbed up on the counter to watch her do her magic. Our kitchen was the largest room in the apartment and was equipped with a large two-door ice box, a big double oven, kerosene cooking stove and plenty of counter space. There was a breakfast nook with a large bay window looking out on the front of the plant that seated four comfortably. A small coal stove for general heating sat near the breakfast nook. This was my favorite place in the entire world.

Tonight we were having fried quail, rice, gravy, butterbeans and homemade biscuits. My grandfather and his hunting buddy, Ed Rule, had killed the birds this afternoon. Crip had carefully picked and cleaned them. My grandmother would soak them in eggs and buttermilk, coat them with a mixture of flour, salt and pepper and fry them in her large black iron skillet with Crisco and bacon grease. Served with homemade biscuits, country butter and watermelon rind preserves. I suspect this is what God had for supper.

While she prepared the meal, I sat propped against the cabinets engulfed in a sea of wonderful aromas; quail frying and biscuits baking, accented by the rich whiskey smell of fruitcake that had been soaking since August. The coal stove had the kitchen comfortably warm in spite of the icy wind blowing snow and sleet just outside the bay window. Bing Crosby was singing White Christmas on the radio. I have never since felt as happy, safe and secure as I did that winter evening in 1944.

Soon supper was ready, and we all gathered at the table to enjoy a meal so wonderful that I can taste, smell and remember it to this very day. My grandfather talked about the war and the effect rationing was having on business in general. We were fortunate. Our business was considered to be essential to the war effort, and we were exempt from many of the restrictions placed on ordinary people. We could get all of the gasoline and tires that were needed to keep the trucks rolling, and clearly we did not have to worry about coal for heat; we had 100 tons or more piled in huge mounds just behind the plant.

After dinner I helped my grandmother clean the kitchen while my grandfather moved to the small living room to read his evening newspaper. We got the Memphis Commercial Appeal in the morning and the Memphis Press Scimitar in the afternoon. Cumberland was equidistant from Jackson, Mississippi's state capital, and Memphis, the world center of the cotton business. We seldom went to Jackson, but we went to Memphis regularly for shopping and many of the services that life required.

After we cleaned the kitchen, my grandmother and I joined my grandfather in the cozy little living room. Later in the evening my grandmother would convert the couch to my bed, and this would be my bedroom. There was a large jacketed coal-burning heater on the back wall of the room that retained enough residual heat to warm the whole apartment until a new fire could be lit early the next morning. I went to sleep listening to the pops and pings of the heater cooling down, and woke every morning as my grandfather lit the kindling for a new day.

Tonight the living room was decorated for the holidays. There was a six foot high Christmas tree decorated with those old triangular-shaped colored bulbs, if one went out, they all went out. There were red, green, silver and gold glass balls along with tin foil icicles. My grandmother had put red and green paper garlands around the ceiling. Folding red paper bells were placed strategically about, and there was a layer of real cotton posing as snow under the tree.

In addition to the big heater there was a large console-size Emerson radio against the opposite wall. This evening would be special. My grandfather begin to tune the Emerson to one of the 50,000 watt clear channel stations in the South. WWL in New Orleans was our favorite. If reception was bad on that frequency, we would try WSB in Atlanta or WSM in Chicago. In the summer we listened to the St. Louis Cardinals on KMOX. We would listen to today's news on CBS with H.V. Kaltenborn, and there was a special Christmas Edition of Your Hit Parade. Our evening was set.

At 7:00 pm the CBS news came on, and Mr. Kaltenborn went immediately to the war. The Nazis had punched a huge hole in the American lines in Belgium, and the only thing keeping them from pouring through to the English Channel was a small garrison of paratroopers in a little village called *Bastogne*. The paratroopers refused to yield, and the whole German offensive was being delayed. General Eisenhower had dispatched General George Patton's Third American Army to relieve the airborne soldiers, and he was moving an entire Army through the worst winter in recent European history. The whole thing was called the 'Battle of the Bulge', and it was hanging by a thread.

The only other news I can remember had something to do with another strike by the United Mine Workers, John L. Lewis, which seemed to really aggravate President Roosevelt. It irritated my grandfather as well. He didn't like anything that messed with the price of coal. Finally, Mr. Kaltenborn made his way through the news and the Lucky Strike theme song came on telling us that *Your Hit Parade* was on the air.

Intermixed with comments about Lucky Strike going to war in a green package, many of America's top entertainers sang all of the old favorite Christmas Carols, plus several newer hits such as *The Christmas Song* about chestnuts roasting on an open fire and two that I loved; *Rudolph The Red Nosed Reindeer* and *Santa Claus Is Coming to Town*. By the time Frank Sinatra sang his version of *White Christmas*, I was drifting off to sleep.

I sat in my grandfather's lap while my grandmother made up my bed. I was soon fast asleep. They stayed up a while, had a piece of the fruitcake and a final cup of coffee. When they were sure I was not going to wake up, they put my presents under the tree. The wind howled, the snow and sleet swirled, the stove crackled and groaned and I slept all night.

Lights On The Levee

My grandmother shook me awake and handed me a cup of hot cocoa. It was pitch black outside the ice plant, and a hoary spangle of frost spread across the windows. I sat groggily on the edge of my bed and tried to remember just why we were getting up in the middle of a freezing winter night. I took a sip of my hot chocolate and saw my grandfather, dressed in his hunting clothes, stacking bricks on top of the coal stove that heated our apartment. Then I remembered; we were going duck hunting on the oxbow lake at Benoit. I jumped off the bed and began putting on the hunting gear my grandmother had laid out on the chair next to my bed. It was mid December of 1947, and I had just turned eight years old that September. This was going to be my first real duck hunt.

Most of my hunting clothes were my grandfather's hand-me-downs. He was a small man, about 5 foot nine and maybe 120 pounds. He was wiry and strong. With a little stitch here and there, I could fit into his castoffs. I pulled on long underwear, two pairs of wool socks, canvas pants and a wool shirt. I then struggled into a wool sweater and rubber boots.

When my grandfather got up early to go hunting or fishing, my grandmother would get up thirty minutes earlier to get the kitchen warm and begin breakfast. I could smell bacon frying and the rich aroma of freshly brewed coffee. There were plates of fried eggs at everyone's place and a platter of steaming fresh homemade biscuits in the center. Breakfast was ready!

Once my grandfather joined us and we said grace, I took a biscuit, split it and smeared a large chunk of homemade country butter between the halves. When the country-cured thick-sliced bacon was passed, I took two pieces. I was allowed to have coffee every morning, and I laced mine with condensed milk. I finished my meal with a second big biscuit and a healthy dollop of homemade watermelon rind preserves.

My grandmother was splitting the rest of the biscuits and stuffing them with the remaining bacon. We would have a mid-morning snack in our duck blind. She filled a large thermos with scalding hot coffee and another one with ice cold milk. She wanted to make sure we were properly provisioned. My grandfather packed the goodies in an old tackle box and we began loading the rest of our gear.

A new pickup truck had been on order since the end of World War II and would be delivered soon. Until then we were stuck with the old truck. Diamond T made all of the ice plant's big, heavy duty delivery trucks, and the dealer in Memphis had made sure that we would get one of the first built as soon as postwar production started. The new one would have a heater, which was certainly going to be a big improvement. Until it was delivered we would heat the old truck with the bricks warming on the stove top. Pa would wrap them in a flannel cloth and I would prop my stocking feet on them. Believe it or not, they would keep me warm all the way to Benoit.

During the loading process I had two responsibilities: take care of my own gear and make sure the decoys were loaded in the boat. I watched as the night foreman and his helper loaded the small wooden boat into the back of the pickup. Pa had built the boat from some plans in Field and Stream for the ideal floating duck blind. The little green boat was just large enough for two and had steel hoops over its top like a covered wagon. There was a large bale of netting that we used to cover the boat when it was converted to a floating blind.

Once the boat was secured in the truck bed, the men attached a small 5HP Evinrude outboard motor to its stern. I made sure the three big bags of decoys were nestled into the truck bed and would not blow out on the way to the lake. I carefully placed my Fox double- barreled 12 gauge shotgun, secure in its case, under the front seat and checked to be sure I had my hat, gloves and big canvas jacket. We were ready to go.

The windshield of the little truck was frosted with a spider web of geometric ice crystals. The dry arctic air that had come in on yesterday's cold front made bright twinkling stars sparkle with an icy brilliance. The thermometer on the gate to the dog pen had read 19 °F, and the frozen weeds near the parked truck snapped and crackled underfoot . While the arctic air made even the simplest task daunting, it also assured us of plenty of new flight ducks coming down from the Canadian prairies. The leading edge of a cold front always made for the very best duck hunting and this morning was going to be a classic. I could barely conceal my excitement and anticipation.

Everything was loaded up and we gave my grandmother a wave as we crunched out of the gravel parking lot and headed to Highway 8. The night was still dark, as the hour just before dawn usually is. I never really knew why that was so, still don't for that matter, but it is.

We headed West on Highway 8 and soon saw the twinkling lights of Dockery Plantation in the distance. In the Mississippi Delta, even in daytime, it can be very difficult to judge distances. The Delta is a perfectly level alluvial plain reaching two hundred miles from Vicksburg in the south to Memphis in the north and about 80 miles from the Mississippi River to the mid-state hills. Hardwood trees lined the muddy, turgid waters of the bayous that fed the Sunflower and Yazoo Rivers. The only variations in elevation were the railroad embankments and a scattering of ancient Indian mounds. Driving in the Delta was a lot like being at sea.

As we passed through Dockery I noticed that the General Store was already open with a half dozen pickups in the parking lot. We weren't the only folks going hunting this morning. Somewhere in the eight miles between Dockery Plantation and the next little town there was just the hint of a new day in our rear view mirror. We passed through the little village and I noticed lights coming on in almost all of the houses.

In another twenty minutes we reached Rosedale and drove up on to the main levee system. We turned south to follow the levee to Benoit and descended on the river side of the levee along a well-kept gravel road. I noticed a group of bright lights across the Mississippi River along the distant western bank. I was too excited to ask about them.

Soon we entered a cattle gap with a sign announcing the Benoit Hunting and Outing Club and I could see the lights on in the main club house. Inside the rough cypress building sat a dozen men and boys at a long wooden table eating a steaming hot breakfast. My grandfather poured a cup of coffee and took a seat.

"Morning, O.B. , This young fella must be that grandson we've heard so much about," said a big red faced man in hunting gear.

"Morning, y'all. This is my grandson, Tommy. We're about to go on his first real duck hunt."

"Where you planning on hunting this morning, O.B.?"

"Thought we'd go across the lake and find a spot along the bank where the water is protected and open. Oughta be a good morning for flight ducks."

"Well, it's damn sure cold enough; there's ice all along the edge of the lake. "

After a little more polite conversation, we excused ourselves and went back into the frigid dawn. Pa backed the pickup down the gravel boat ramp where he and two of the club's outside men set the boat in the water with its bow on dry land

We loaded our gear, and were ready to go. Pa got in the boat and moved to the stern to operate the motor, and I climbed in the front and settled down on the little wooden slat that served as a seat. The cold air was filled with the unforgettable smell of outboard motor fuel and wood smoke. One of the men pushed us off the gravel, as Pa cranked the little motor.

We started across the lake as the sky in the east began to turn from dim blues and purples to yellows and pinks. There was just enough light to see the dark trees lining the lakeside and only the brightest stars were still visible. It only took a couple of minutes to cross the lake to the opposite bank and soon we were idling along the shoreline looking for just the right spot. It wasn't long before we pulled into a small bay of water that was protected from the wind by the large trees lining the lake.

Pa tied one end of the boat to a sapling and I looped a line around a stump near my end. The sun had yet to peek over the distant levee, but there was now enough light to see to shoot. While Pa waded out to set the decoys, I looked up into the morning sky and could see large V's of migrating ducks heading south. I could barely make out their distant chatter. I have never again seen as many ducks and geese at one time; the sky was filled with their formations as they looked for a place to feed.

Once the decoys had been set, we pulled the netting over the back and top of the blind, leaving an opening facing the lake. Pa took out two large coffee cans containing a roll of toilet paper soaked in kerosene. He struck a wooden match and lit both cans and handed one to me.

"Put this down on the bottom of the boat and try not to kick it over when the shooting starts," he said.

There was a bright blue flame and wiggly visible heat rising from the cans. They provided an amazing amount of warmth. I uncased my gun and slipped two #4 high brass shells into the double barrel, closed the breech and pushed on the safety. Let the hunt begin.

There is a magic moment that defines the joy of hunting and is the real reason we all keep coming back and it has nothing to do with killing game. In every type of hunting I have ever done this moment comes when the hunter has gotten into position, be it in a duck blind, a tree stand or sitting on a log squirrel hunting. This moment happens in the lull that allows nature to settle back to normal after man has violated its tranquility and order.

I can remember looking over the spread of decoys as the sun rose across the lake and the sky filled with thousands of waterfowl and thinking that this was the prettiest sight I had ever seen. My reverie was shattered by the raucous squawk of Pa's duck call sounding the high ball to get the attention of a flight of ducks high above us.

I knew better than to look up to see what was going on. I just watched Pa as he began to work the ducks. I could tell he had been successful in turning the flight of ducks our way when he switched to the twittering sound of the feed call. I switched off the safety on my gun and watched Pa's eyes as he worked the wily birds. He dipped his head down, hit the call one last time and gave me the go ahead look.

I raised my shotgun and saw about twenty canvas backs filling the sky in front of the blind. The ducks all had their wings cupped to land in our spread of decoys, and as we moved they all began to flap their wings furiously in an attempt to regain airspeed and flee to safety. I heard Pa's gun fire two quick shots and watched as two ducks splashed into the lake. The remaining birds were beating their wings and moving out of range. I had forgotten to shoot.

Pa reloaded his gun and I put my safety back on while his eyes turned skyward again. Soon he was working another flock within shooting range. Pa got two more, and I shot a duck that could not have been more than ten feet away which crumpled just outside the blind. Pa coaxed the floating drake Canvasback to the side of the blind with his sculling paddle and waited for me to pick it up. I place it in the gunny sack we brought to haul the fruits of our morning.

"Nice shot," he said, "you might want to pick one a little further out, your shot string will be a little bigger and you won't riddle him with so much lead."

"Yes sir," I grinned, "he was about all I could see."

The ducks continued to fly for about another half hour or so and Pa killed six more, four Mallards and two Gadwalls. I managed to hit a Mallard hen, which I know irritated Pa, but he didn't say anything. The legal limit was twelve ducks apiece and we were about half way there when the flight ducks found a place to feed and the sky was empty of birds. It was time to have a little snack, but first we would pick up the dead birds.

We untied the blind, and using the sculling paddle Pa expertly maneuvered to each bird which I picked up and put in the gunny sack. We had a total of eleven ducks in the bag as we retied the blind back into position. Pa pulled out the tackle box and handed me a biscuit and bacon along with the thermos of cold milk.

"Son, you won't see many mornings any better than this one," he said between bites of biscuits and sips of coffee, "You just can't beat the leading edge of a cold front for ducks. Don't expect every hunt to be like this. Now that the flight ducks are feeding, we'll have to work hard to fill our limit."

"If I'm ever going to be any good at this, you better teach me how to use a duck call. Every shot we got was on a flight that you called in. Think I could learn to call?"

Before he could comment, two Mallards whistled just over our head and landed in the decoys. I was reaching for my gun when Pa shook his head from side to side. I put the gun down and mouthed a silent "why?"

He put his finger to his lips and whispered, "Just enjoy watching them swim around and learn a little about their ways."

We watched the pair of green headed drakes dabble and chatter for about five minutes and then Pa clapped his hands and they streaked across the water leaving a tail of spray until they grabbed enough air and took off for parts unknown.

I looked at Pa and asked, "Why didn't we shoot them? We could have gotten both."

"Son, this is a sport and it's about sharing the morning with nature and matching wits with one of the savviest creatures on God's earth. It's not about killing. I want to teach you to be a sportsman and a gentleman, and neither would shoot a duck on the water. If you are ever hunting with someone who does, take him off your list of hunting companions, and always be careful of any dealings with him."

We sat silently while I gave this some serious thought and then said. "I think I see what you mean about it not being about killing; it's sort of like why we never shoot out a covey of quail. It just wouldn't be right for the birds."

Pa looked at me and smiled, "Yeah, it's pretty much the same thing. Don't kill over the legal limit, don't shoot doves over a baited field and don't shoot a doe. There are two good reasons for all of these rules; they are the right thing to do, and they assure that we will continue to have animals and birds to hunt. This is why I send a donation to Ducks Unlimited every year; they are working in Canada to assure that we have ducks far into the future."

"Well, it must be working; there were ducks and geese all over the place this morning."

"Like I said, don't expect this every time you go."

Pa was dead on about having to work for the rest of our limit. He managed to call a couple of flights of a half dozen or less into shooting range and we banged away at maybe a dozen singles. Pa killed eight more birds, and I wasted a half box of shells punching holes in the sky. Hitting a fast flying duck with a winter tail wind is best left to expert wing shots. Pa could hold his own in that league.

About eleven o'clock we gathered up the decoys and headed back across the lake to the club landing. While Pa and the outside guys pulled the boat out and put it in the bed of the truck, I went inside to use the bathroom. The cooks were preparing fried chicken for lunch and the whole place smelled wonderful.

I walked over to the kitchen area and smiled at the black guy frying the chicken in a huge cast-iron skillet. He looked and me, grinned and said, "Bet you could eat a drumstick this morning."

"I sure could," I answered as he picked a freshly cooked leg and wrapped it in a napkin. "Thanks" I said and went back outside gnawing away on the drumstick.

"Did you stow your gun?" Pa asked.

"It's in its case under the seat." I replied.

"Well, I guess we're ready to head back, let me visit the men's room and we'll hit the road."

"Better check out that fried chicken, it's mighty tasty."

"I may just do that," he said as he headed to the club house.

I sat on a wooden bench beside the door, leaned back and looked at the bright blue sky. The cold front had cleared all of the cloud cover and the air smelled clean and crisp. The sun warmed my little spot, and before I knew it, I was sound asleep.

Pa slammed the screen door just a little harder than absolutely necessary and I woke instantly.

"You ready to go?" he asked.

"I stifled a yawn and said, "Yep, I was just resting my eyes.""

That's what Pa always said when he fell asleep listening to the radio.

We started back down the gravel access road to the main levee system and soon were high above ground level with a great view in all directions. We passed through a cattle gap and Pa pulled the truck over to the side of the levee road.

"Look across the river," he said, pointing to the Louisiana side. "What do you see?"

I looked where he was pointing and realized it was where I'd seen all the lights as we came in this morning. I could see large cranes and other construction equipment working furiously.

"I'm not sure; looks like they are building something on the river bank." I replied.

"That's a natural gas pipeline and it will be across the river by early spring. That source of cheap natural gas, along with the growing production of reasonably priced refrigerators, spells the death of the ice and coal business. We were fortunate during the war, but I'm afraid it's going to be all downhill from now on."

"What'll we do?"

"I've had an offer to sell the plant to Crystal Ice & Coal out of Memphis, and I think I'm gonna let em have it while the price is at the top. A year from now I won't be able to give it away."

And that is exactly what he did. By the time for spring planting Pa had re-invested the money he made from selling the ice plant and bought 3600 acres of prime Sunflower County cotton land. He rented the land to one of his good farmer friends for the next crop year, and we moved to a small house out on the Quiver River about 6 miles east of Cumberland.

All of Pa's buddies that met every morning at Eddie's Café for coffee assured him that he would lose his shirt trying to farm. This prediction was based on the fact that Pa had never grown tomatoes, let alone cotton. His answer was,

"How hard can it be? You guys are doing it."

Just to hedge his bets, he enrolled as a student at Mississippi State College in Starkville, Mississippi's Land Grant school, and spent a year in a crash course on modern farming techniques. In 1949, he had the most fiber per acre in the Delta, averaging 1376 pounds. And the next thing you know we became farmers.

Bobbie Jean's Boobs

Benny and I were lying on his sleeping porch with a huge floor fan pushing the damp Delta air directly on us. The fan not only stirred the hot humid air, but filled the porch with the bouquet of honeysuckle and Confederate Jasmine. The radio in the living room droned through the open window, and Harry Caray told us Stan Musial had hit a two-RBI double to put the Cards back in the lead. We recognized this as a temporary situation. It was early August and St. Louis was pretty much out of the pennant race. Musial was having a great year, but even Stan the Man couldn't carry a load like these hapless Red Birds. They looked a lot like the old St. Louis Browns.

We had wolfed down a huge dinner at noon, and along with every other sane person in Cumberland, Mississippi, we retired to the sleeping porch to avoid the heat and humidity. We drifted on the edge of consciousness, serenaded by the murmur of insects, birds and the comforting play-by-play of Harry Caray. Even with the fan it was too hot to sleep; we just lay there, sweating in a chicken and dumpling stupor. There had been a polio epidemic in the summer of 1952, and our parents insisted that we keep still and indoors until it began to cool off. The term "cool off" is relative in the Mississippi Delta during August. If 100 °F and 96% humidity at 1:00 was the norm, then 94 °F and 87% humidity at 3:00 really did qualify as cooling off. Benny's home was nestled in a grove of cottonwood trees, and their cooling shade was worth a 20 degree respite from the relentless summer sun.

We could usually escape our "polio prison" around 2:30 or so, and we were discussing our next move. Benny was in favor of going downtown and sitting in Flower's air conditioned Drug Store to sneak a peek at the latest comic books. He knew my grandmother had given me a quarter this morning and figured we could afford a couple of fountain Cokes. While Benny's plan had the advantage of comfort and safety, I was pushing for a more daring course of action.

I thought we should sneak behind Mrs. Denson's house and climb up on her garage roof. We could ease over the military crest of her old shingled garage and be safe from discovery from all directions. Once in position, we would have a perfect trajectory to see into Bobbie Jean Cole's bathroom. We knew from past scouting trips that Bobbie Jean's mother would insist that she take her afternoon bath when she completed her polio sentence. In spite of a few intervening branches, vines and a less than transparent window screen, we could see enough to make the effort worthwhile.

Benny was mounting a spirited defense of the air conditioned drug store plan when I played my trump card. I told him that I had smuggled my Grandfather's World War I Navy binoculars out of the house this morning and hidden them under the juniper bush in Mrs. Denson's side yard.

"No shit! You really got 'em?"

"You know it, and according to Pa you can see the hairs on a German's balls from half a mile away."

"I don't really much care about any German's balls, but I have a great deal of interest in any hair that Bobbie Jean might be sporting."

"I wouldn't mind a clear view of those little tits she's so proud of. Whadda ya say?"

I could see the gleam of lust in his eyes, and I knew I had carried the day. As soon as we could spring ourselves from captivity we'd be off to see Cumberland's answer to the Seven Wonders of the World, Bobbie Jean Cole naked.

Benny couldn't stand it any longer. He raced inside and found his mother in the kitchen. He told her he was worried that the Bowman's Holstein, Myrtle, which was pastured across the railroad tracks, and would need fresh water on a scorcher like today. She just shook her head and said it was a fine idea. Benny was the youngest of four brothers and there was hardly a line his mother hadn't heard before. We were free.

We jumped off the porch and raced across the tracks to bring relief to Myrtle. The water supply was in fine shape, but we took the hose and topped it off just in case. We decided to spray each other just to cool off. It was so damn hot that our shorts and tee

21

shirts would dry in minutes. As we started our return trip over the tracks, we heard the long low moan of a train whistle and looked north to see the afternoon freight chugging into sight.

This presented one of those judgment dilemmas that so often confound twelve-year-old boys. There were not many hard fast rules of engagement in our world, but one of the chief no-no's concerned on- coming trains. The rule was this: If you could hear the whistle or see the smoke, don't cross the tracks. Wait until the train passes. This was a clear cut case of overkill in our estimation. You could hear the whistle and see the smoke a mile or more away.

The Mississippi Delta is a totally flat alluvial plain. If there were no trees or if the track didn't bend, you could probably see the damn train when it left Memphis. It made no sense to wait 10 minutes to cross 25 feet of space to avoid something that was a mile away. This ridiculous piece of legislation had been unanimously adopted after that dumbass Ricky Evans had decided he could out run the Illinois Central's City of New Orleans to the main crossing in Cumberland. He lost the race, his bicycle and his left foot.

We knew Bobbie Jean's bath time was fast approaching, and she didn't linger; she bathed and got out. We had a very narrow window in which to work. On the other hand, my grandmother had a distant view of our current position. Benny's mother had an even better one, and Mrs. Denson was probably watching, eager to rat us out. If Bobbie Jean finishes her bath we are faced with at least a 24-hour delay. If we get caught crossing the tracks ahead of the train we get the crap beat out of us.

We sprinted across the tracks at full speed and headed toward Mrs. Denson's juniper bush to retrieve the glasses. I grabbed a low hanging branch on the chinaberry tree growing next to Mrs. Denson's garage and pulled myself onto the interior limb structure of the tree. I climbed up high enough to jump across to the garage roof, and Benny followed. We slid down below the roof line and made ourselves as inconspicuous as possible. The game was on.

I removed the binocular strap from around my neck and began to focus on the Cole's bathroom window. Pa was right about these glasses, they were high quality German military issue and their resolution at 75 feet was amazing. I focused on a bar of soap on the edge of the bathtub and could clearly read "Lifebuoy". This was gonna be outstanding.

We had just settled into our concealed position when a car pulled into the Cole's driveway. Bobbie Jean's gray haired grandmother got out of the car and went in the side door. Soon after she came back out accompanied by Bobbie Jean, who was carrying one of those little square suitcases that girls seemed to favor. She was clearly going to spend the night at her grandmother's house.

"Aw shit," Benny exclaimed, "Can you believe it?"

"Well, there's not a hellava lot we can do about it. At least we had a chance to test the equipment," I said, lowering the binoculars and replacing them around my neck. "Tomorrow is another day."

"Thanks, Scarlett, I feel so much better now."

Benny and I were sitting there deep in dejection when we saw a movement in Mrs. Denson's backyard. We crouched down close to the shingles and held our breath. The last thing we needed was to get caught looking in the Cole's bathroom window. I didn't want to contemplate Benny's father's reaction when someone called for police back up. He was not known for a great sense of humor and did not buy into the "boys will be boys" school of discipline. He was more the "spare the rod, spoil the child" type. My grandmother would just have a duck.

We sat as still as death and watching Benny's big brother Ron slip through a hole in the fence and trot across the Cole's backyard. He quietly climbed the back steps and gently knocked on the kitchen door. Bobbie Jean's mother came to the door and quickly let him in. The kitchen door had barely clicked when Ron and Mrs. Cole were in a frantic embrace. I looked at Benny and he looked at me. We were speechless.

I pulled the binoculars from around my neck and quickly focused on the kitchen window. Ron had his tongue down Ms. Cole's throat and his hand under her dress grasping at God only knows what. I could not believe what I was seeing. I gave the glasses to Benny and he damn near fell off the roof. Conventional wisdom dictated that this was the perfect time to make a clean get away. The last time I screwed around with Ron, he nailed me with a claw hammer as I ran toward my grandmother's house in terror. It was a heck of a throw, fifty feet on a dead run and a clean shot to the back of my head. I found myself rubbing the dent in my skull, and fighting an urge to get the hell out of Dodge.

We were confident that if Ron ever found out what we were seeing , he would kill both of us without hesitation. I knew this and Benny, who basically was not scared on a soul on this earth, knew I was right. But we couldn't move. We just handed the glasses back and forth until the panting couple disappeared into another room. We finally allowed ourselves to exhale and allow some of our newly functional hormones to take a break.

"Quit rubbing your stupid head," Benny said. "He can't see us up here."

"That's easy for you to say; he never hit you with a hammer. You don't have to worry. If Ron's hits you, Will and Charlie will whip his butt. Me, he can kill and there's no one to avenge me."

This was not exactly true. You'd rather sandpaper a wildcat's ass than cross my grandmother when it came to my welfare. Ron damn near had to move to Blytheville, Arkansas to live with his uncle till she cooled off about the hammer- throwing incident. In spite of my grandmother's mayhem, I knew I couldn't rat Ron out if he caught us. I'd just have to take my medicine.

We figured the show was over and we were packing up to leave when the light went on in the bathroom. Mrs. Cole came into view and began to undress. I looked at Benny and said, "You want to go?"

He snarled, "Not a chance."

I unstrapped the glasses and focused them on the scene unfolding before us. Bobbie Jean may have some very nice little tits, but her mother had a Boone and Crockett rack - big brown circles with nipples the size of walnuts. Benny and I had copped a look at his sister Rosemary on a couple of occasions, and we had a rudimentary idea of what to expect. But nothing could have prepared us for Mrs. Cole in all of her glory. The glasses flew between us and all of her charms were soon revealed. This could not get better, but it did.

Ron entered the picture, and he was stark naked. It was a well known fact that all of the Bowman boys were uncircumcised and well endowed. Benny and I had seen all three of the older guys changing clothes or bathing. While Charlie and Will were impressive, Ron was in a class all his own. We had figured this out even though we had never seen it angry. Well here it was in a screaming purple rage. Ms. Cole could not keep her hands off it.

I have no idea how long the ensuing tableau took to play out. It could have been five minutes or two hours. We sat on that garage roof and saw the entire Kama Sutra performed in living color. When the participants finally collapsed exhausted into the bathtub, it was as if Benny and I had returned to Earth after an alien abduction. We sat quietly on Mrs. Denson's garage roof, each absorbed in private thoughts.

Viewing the Ron and Mrs. Cole show had been like trying to drink from a fire hose- too much imagery in too short a time. We were in sensory overload. Sweat ran down my face and my breathing had yet to return to normal. Not a word was said. What could you say that would do justice to what we had just witnessed? It was then that I noticed my damp underwear. I had experienced a fully conscious wet dream.

It is widely accepted that the pre-teen brain is not fully functional and can easily be twisted by traumatic events. To say my brain had been impacted is like saying that bombing Pearl Harbor pissed off the United States. I was marked for life. Ron and Ms. Cole set a mark for sexual activity that became my personal Gold

Standard. To this day, a little over sixty years later I can play the whole tape in whatever portion of my brain that houses my libido.

Benny finally spoke.

"I don't think he stuck it in her ear, or did I just miss it?"

"Well, if he didn't it was surely an oversight, he hit every other available target."

I have no idea how much time had passed since we first climbed on to that roof, but when we regained our wits it was starting to get dark. Just as we were starting to leave the roof, Ron opened the Cole's kitchen door, gave Mrs. Cole a perfunctory kiss and eased his way through the back fence. He walked directly to Mrs. Denson's garage and suddenly stopped; he looked up at us as we gasped in terror. Wearing a big grin he said, "You guys see what you came for?"

Ron Bowman remains one of my favorite people to this day. Benny and I never again visited the roof. It was as if we knew that we could never repeat the experience. We had been to the mountain top.

Burning The Boats

Pa and I drove the six miles into Cumberland and parked the pickup in front of Eddie's Café. Breakfast at Eddie's was our Saturday morning routine, that is unless we were going duck hunting or trying to catch some bass before it got too hot. We planned to go bird hunting later in the day, but we had plenty of time for breakfast. Besides, we had other business at Eddie's this morning.

In addition to being the best place to eat breakfast in Cumberland, Eddie's served as the hub of the farmer's information network. When you walked through the door of Eddie's you were greeted by the aroma of freshly brewed coffee, frying bacon, and above all else, the smell of the best pancakes in creation. Eddie had a secret formula for his pancakes that I have never seen replicated. They were light, fluffy and just plain delicious. He also served real country butter and real maple syrup. It was a hard combo to beat.

There were men sitting around two tables in the back drinking coffee and discussing farming and world events. Pa referred to them as the Farmer's Arts and Rural Transcendentalist Society or FARTS for short. They were dressed in vested suits to bib overalls and most everything in between. My grandfather had on his usual uniform, khaki pants, grey work shirt, suspenders and scuffed work boots. The whole ensemble was set off by an old felt hat that was sweat stained and battered. He fit right in. This was a tricky group to assess and a perfect example of the adage that you shouldn't judge a book by its cover.

The men in the suits were local lawyers and a junior banker, and the rest either owned a business or were farmers. A large red faced man in faded bib overalls was Ray Allen Jones who looked like he had just jumped off the morning freight train. In reality he owned and farmed about 16,000 acres of the best cotton land this side of the Nile Valley and had more money than God. He drove a battered and dusty 1939 Ford pickup, but his wife was chauffeured around in a 1948 Lincoln Continental about the size of the USS Coral Sea. In Cumberland looks could be deceiving.

Pa and I took a seat at a table adjacent to the old Farts, and I ordered pancakes and sausage patties while he thumb tacked a notice to the bulletin board. He returned to his seat and placed his order for Cream of Wheat and biscuits. You could see a ripple of curiosity pulse through the group at the other tables, but no one wanted to get up and go read the notice. I knew what it said because I had watched as he printed it in large black letters:

FARM HANDS AVAILABLE

THE O.B. RAINER FARM

SATURDAY, DEC. 10TH 1951

TWENTY-SIX FAMILIES OF PRIME NEGRO FARM HANDS WILL BE AVAILABLE FOR EMPLOYMENT

AT THE QUIVER RIVER FARM OF O.B. RAINER ON SATURDAY, DECEMBER 10, 1951 AT 8:00 AM.

THESE ARE HARD WORKING AND EXPERIENCED FARM HANDS

AND

I RECOMMEND THEM PERSONALLY. THEY WILL BE AN ASSET TO ANY FARMING OPERATION.

O.B. RAINER

Eventually one of the men eased up and walked toward the Men's room and on the way he stopped long enough to read the notice. You could see him stiffen with surprise and hurry back to the table. Soon the entire group of Farts was abuzz with excitement; Pa just ate his Cream of Wheat and read the

Commercial Appeal as if nothing was going on. Finally they couldn't stand it any longer.

"O.B., what made you decide to quit farming? I thought you were doing pretty well," offered Bill Kyle, one of the bigger farmers in the county.

"I am doing well, and as a matter of fact, I have no intention of quitting. Actually, I'll be trying to rent more land next year. Think you might want to cut back some?"

"Well, if I did want to rent some of my land, which by the way I don't, it surely would not be to somebody with no field hands."

"Oh, I'll have plenty of labor; in fact I will have five of my best hands staying with me."

"Five hands, huh? You'll be lucky to farm 100 acres with five hands. How many acres you planning on working?"

"I'll probably work about 3500 total, and like I said, I'd like to rent some more if I could get good land."

"3500 acres with five hands, even you oughta know that's impossible."

"Not if you have the right five hands and the right equipment. I don't anticipate any problems."

"Well, those five hands better be some cotton -chopping and cotton -picking supermen, that's all I've got to say."

"I wish it was all that you had to say, but I know I won't be that lucky. You oughta come and pick up some of my excess hands next Saturday; you can always use more labor, can't you?"

"I might just do that. Your hands must be something else if you are going to farm 3500 acres with five of them. I oughta take them all and farm all of Sunflower County."

"I'd talk to Ray Allen before I started farming all of Sunflower County, since he owns most of it. That is unless you're looking for a farm managers job, Ray Allen might be interested in hiring you. "

"You can bet your ass that I'll go to Detroit and build Fords before I'd work for Ray Allen Jones."

"You can double down on that bet," said Ray Allen, "I'd take a sulfuric acid enema before I'd hire Billy Kyle to feed my bird dogs, let alone manage my little farming operation."

That brought the house down with guffaws of raucous laughter and a general relaxing of the air of tension that had been building. People got up and paid their tabs and headed to the door, even cotton farmers had to do something vaguely resembling work. Ray Allen Jones came over and pulled up a chair. He truly didn't have to work.

"O.B., just what in the hell are you up to?" he asked.

"Nothing sinister, Ray Allen, just gettin' ready for next year's plantin'."

"I know you. We've been on the Board at Cumberland Planters Bank together for nearly twenty years. I have a great deal of respect for your business acumen, and I'm one of the few people that think you know something about farming. I'd really be interested in what you are planning to do."

"It's pretty simple. I plan to be fully mechanized next year. I'm buying three big John Deeres and two of the new cotton pickers. I kept my best hands and put them on weekly salary and a profit sharing plan. I believe the five of them can get my crop in and picked. I'll pick up some day labor if I need 'em."

"Hands on a salary and profit sharing, some of the boys ain't gonna like that idea. Fact is, I'm not so sure I like it very much."

"Stop and think about it Ray Allen, the war changed America. Negroes served in combat roles for the first time since the Indian Wars. They're fighting in Korea right now. If it was hard to keep

31

the whites down on the farm after they saw Paree in 1918, it will be impossible to expect the Negroes to be willing to accept the sharecropper system much longer. Change is coming and I want to get ahead of it. Besides, the old sharecropper system doesn't really work with modern agriculture any more than slavery was working in 1860."

"You really believe we'll have trouble with the Negroes?"

"I'm not saying there'll be race riots or anything like that, but I do believe that the Negroes will start to organize and demand better wages and living conditions. Hell, Ray Allen, they're living in uninsulated shacks with no running water and using an outhouse. This is the middle of the 20th Century and that won't work much longer. I want to have some reliable hands that will be on the leading edge of the coming changes."

"I still think you are over-reacting O.B., the Negroes have always been satisfied with the way things are. I think they really like not having any real responsibility. They are pretty simple folks."

"They may be simple, but they're not stupid. I don't think the present system will last another ten years, but what do I know? I've made my decision based on what I see coming. I certainly don't expect anyone else to follow suit."

"Well, it gives me something to think about. You were right about selling the Ice and Coal business in '47; you really did get top dollar and now it looks like they'll be closing up if things don't get better quick. You were also right about planting that Georgia hybrid cotton; it has really made a difference in our yields."

"Ray Allen, you are the only big farmer that switched to the hybrid seed; the rest of them would rather get lower yields than try something new. They'll hang on to the sharecropper system until all the hands have gone to Detroit to work in the auto plants. Then they'll have no choice. You ought to mechanize now and get your cost in line before you have to."

"Like I said, O.B., you've given me something to think about. Gotta run and check on my fields. See you in the morning."

After Mr. Jones had gone, I looked at my grandfather and said,

"Pa, do you think he will do it?"

"Probably not this coming year, but he'll be one of the first to face the coming reality. Let's go bird hunting this afternoon and see what we can scare up."

I thought that was a swell plan.

As soon as Pa finished his post-dinner cake and coffee, we began to gather our gear to go bird hunting. I put on a pair of Pa's old canvas brush pants that my grandmother had cut down to fit. I tucked in a flannel shirt and pulled the wide suspenders over my shoulders. I pulled on a pair of boots with rubber bottoms and leather uppers and laced them tight, grabbed my canvas hunting coat and hat. I was ready to go.

I met Pa at the dog pen and he decided to use Lemon, our yellow English setter this afternoon. Lemon meant that we were going to hunt easy. If we were seriously after a limit of birds we would be loading Bill and Bob, our two liver and white pointers. These two were first class bird dogs; both were from the same litter, sired by Texas Ranger, the world field trial champion. Lemon would hunt in close and find the easy coveys. Bill and Bob would range out as far as a half mile in front of the guns and pretty much find every covey out there.

A hunt with Lemon was always a lot of fun. Pa would be relaxed and talkative. We would stroll along behind the dog and take what nature and Lemon would give us. We would kill birds, but not as many.

On the other hand a hunt with the pointers was a whole different deal. The difference started when you let the dogs out of their carrying kennel in the back of the pickup. Lemon would jump down with a lot of tail wagging and nuzzling. He would circle the truck a couple of times, mark his territory and be ready to hunt when we gave the signal. We were in charge of the hunt.

The pointers would hit the ground on a dead run and their circle might have a radius of a quarter of a mile. When they finished their pre-hunt ritual they took off to hunt on their own with no concern about the humans trailing in their wake. You didn't stroll behind pointers like Bob and Bill; you double timed and sometimes broke into a trot. They were in charge of the hunt.

The pace and range of the hunt were major differences, but the main difference was my grandfather's level of intensity. I mentioned that he was relaxed and talkative with Lemon. With the pointers he was intense and focused. If I missed on the covey rise with the setter, he would just smile and shake his head. If I missed with the pointers, I could at best expect a frosty frown and at worst another lecture about letting the damn birds get out into your shot string and don't snap shoot. This afternoon's hunt would be fun.

Today we were going to hunt along the banks of the Quiver River that formed the eastern boundary of our property. We owned about a half mile of river front, and had permission to hunt from our neighboring farmers. We had plenty of prime quail cover to work.

After we loaded our gear and the dog we headed to Toby's house. The afternoon sky was the slate gray of winter with a light breeze out of the west. The gravel road led through acres of gray cotton fields that had been turned under for the season, and the two shades of gray blended at the horizon. You could literally see for miles, and the only things interrupting your view would be the bare black tree lines along the creek banks or an occasional railroad embankment.

In about a half mile we left the gravel and turned down a hard packed dirt road that cut through the fields and ended at a sharecropper's house. The house was made of rough cut cypress planks that over the years had turned a sliver gray. There was a crude brick chimney with a wisp of gray smoke being blown by the light breeze. The house was square shaped and had one front door and two windows opening onto a front porch spanning the width of the structure. It had a rusted tin roof and silver gray outhouse in the back.

We parked in front of the house and walked around to use the back door. At first this puzzled me and I asked Pa why we didn't use the front door. He replied that it was a matter of respect. He expected his Negroes to come to his back door if they had business at our house and he was merely returning the courtesy. This was just one of the many nuances of being the minority ruling class in a society that was ninety-five percent Negro.

Pa said that the system worked because it had a set of customs and rules to ease the friction between the races. I once asked him who developed these customs and rules and his reply was,

"Don't be an idiot, of course we made them. Negroes can't think such things through."

Like the song from South Pacific says, "You have to be carefully taught"; such things are not always intuitive. I did know this; if these customs and rules were relaxed our society would began to unravel. Next thing you know, Negroes would be using our restrooms, drinking from our fountains and sitting in our part of the Delta Theatre watching Tom Mix and Lash LaRue. Better they stay in the balcony.

As we rounded the house I saw the chicken coops, hog pens and a large plowed area green with collard green plants. There was a huge black cast iron cauldron sitting atop a smoldering wood fire. I looked inside and saw overalls and long underwear gently boiling. Pa climbed onto the small uncovered back porch and gently tapped on the door.

Toby's wife, Anna, opened the door and said, "Why, Mistah Rainer, it sho is good to see you. Won't you and the boy come in and let me fix you a little something?"

As we stepped through the door into the kitchen area of the house the first thing I noticed was the dimly lit flicker of kerosene lanterns. The walls were covered by layer upon layer of newspapers that had been glued up and there was the pungent smell of coal smoke, kerosene, frying food and a strange, but not unpleasant, whiff of bodies living in close contact.

Toby rose from the kitchen table and shooed about a half dozen children ranging in age from 2 to 13 or so into the front of the house.

"Mistah Rainer, won't you and Tommy have a little somethin to eat? Anna made some mighty fine biscuits this mornin' and the coffee is fresh made."

"Why, that's mighty nice of you to offer, Toby, and I know all about Anna's biscuits, but I was hoping you would be able to go bird hunting with us this afternoon."

I watched and listened as this very formal tableau was played out. Going to the back door, being invited in and offered coffee and biscuits, even the invitation to go hunting, which we all understood to be more than a suggestion. Here were the manners and customs of our world assuring that neither party lost face or seemed to be coerced. This was the lubricant that eased the friction that very easily could bring the whole system down.

Toby seemed genuinely glad for the opportunity to join us in the hunt. He loved to work the dogs and was certainly their main caregiver and trainer. Pa said that Toby knew more about bird dogs and quail hunting than any one he had ever known.

When Pa was hunting with his farmer buddies, he would never ask Toby to come along. He did not want them to treat Toby like a servant or hired hand. Anytime we hunted by ourselves, Toby would be there, working the dogs and making sure they found birds. I was pretty confident that Toby and Anna would not be among the families displaced by our upcoming mechanization.

Toby grabbed his coat and pulled on his knee-high rubber boots and we all got back in the pickup with me sitting in the middle. We bumped along a turn row and angled toward the tree line that bordered the Quiver River.

"Toby, where you reckon the birds are gonna be this afternoon?" Pa asked as we neared the river.

"Well, suh, it seems to me that we might find them in the light brush along the river bank. They probably be conveyed up resting before they go back to feeding near sundown. We gonna be shootin' any singles this afternoon?"

Toby knew my grandfather hated to shoot the singles after a covey rise. He felt that they should be left alone to assure that you didn't shoot out the covey. If you didn't scatter the birds all over the place they would covey back up and be there the next time you came.

"No, I believe we'll just take what we can from the covey rises, and let the others have a rest."

This was a conversation that would never take place today. There are so few wild birds that the idea you could kill your limit just shooting the covey rise would be pure fantasy. In 1950 we would expect to flush anywhere from six to ten coveys of quail in a morning's hunt and that many or more in the afternoon.

Today there are very few wild quail. Rachel Carson, in her book, Silent Spring blamed DDT and the use of other pesticides and they probably played a part, but I think that the loss of cover and food plots due to creek-bank to creek-bank farming were the real culprits. No cover and no food resulted in no quail.

We parked the truck in the yard of an abandoned sharecropper house that was falling in on itself. Tall weeds grew up all around it while a gone-to-seed chinaberry tree hung on for dear life. When we got out of the truck, I noticed a definite drop in the temperature. The wind had switched from west to north and had the feel of a winter storm coming.

I was leaning against the back fender of the truck and Toby was letting Lemon out of the large dog carrier in the truck bed. Lemon hit the ground and started his circle of the old house. He had gone about twenty five feet when he stopped like he had been pole-axed and froze in a quivering point. There was no mistaking his stance; he was dead in the middle of a covey of quail.

Pa and I looked at one another and he broke his Beretta over and under and placed two shells in the open barrels. I did the same on my Fox double barrel. Toby had moved up behind the shaking dog and was soothing him with a low voice saying,

"Whoa, boy, whoa boy," over and over.

Judging from the stance of the dog and the direction of the wind it was pretty clear that the birds were bunched up in knee high grass between the old house and the ramshackle outhouse. This gave us ample room to position ourselves for the covey rise.

Pa cut his eyes to my left, and I knew that he wanted me to take everything from the center line between us all the way to the house. He would take everything to the right. Neither of us would shoot a bird that flew over the centerline into the other shooters area. This made for very efficient shooting and prevented accidents that might prove fatal.

Toby held Lemon in check and Pa and I slowly moved past the dog and into the grassy area.

What happened next defies description. Some twenty or more bobwhite quail burst from the ground in a 360 degree explosion: blurs of flying birds coming at you from all angles and the intense noise of forty or so frantically flapping wings trying to gain purchase in the cold winter air.

I fought the instinctive reaction to shoot at the closest bird, but kept my attention tightly focused on two birds rapidly moving to my left. I let them get out about thirty feet and fired my first barrel. One of the birds crumpled and fell, and I moved further to my left and fired the other barrel. The second bird seemed to stall in mid air and sailed on cupped wings to the ground about sixty feet out in the cotton stubble.

In all of the excitement of the covey rise I had not even heard Pa shoot, but I knew without asking that he had at least two quail down and I watched Lemon begin his retrieval. Using a combination of vocal commands and hand signals Toby guided Lemon to the three dead birds before he addressed my second shot.

If I had just powdered the quail's tail with random shot the wounded bird could and would run half way to hell before he died.

I was lucky this afternoon, the bird was dead at the end of his glide and Lemon found him with no problem. We would all be eating quail for supper. The weather was progressively getting colder and I suspected it might reach freezing before we finished our hunt.

One of the main reasons my grandmother's fried quail was legendary had nothing to do with how she cooked them, but everything to do with how birds were treated after they were bagged. Toby always carried a ten pound paper ice bag with him. If the weather was warm he would put a pound or so of ice in the insulated bag. When the dog retrieved the bird, Toby would take his penknife and gut them and make a quick check on what they had in their craw.

This would make sure the birds did not start to spoil with ruptured guts and broken bladders, and it would also let us know what they had been eating earlier in the day giving us a clue to where we might find them later. Once field dressed they went into the insulated bag and into the game pouch on Toby's hunting jacket.

We flushed a couple of more coveys along the river bank just as Toby had predicted. I killed two more and Pa got his usual two per covey. We were closing in on a pretty good hunt when the clouds turned a dirty dark gray and seemed to get closer to the ground. Sleet started to rattle off our hats and jackets and the wind moaned as it blew through the leafless trees that lined the river. Quail were pretty darn hard to hit in the best of conditions, but when assisted by a thirty-mile-per hour tail wind, they were nearly impossible.

The weather didn't seem to bother Lemon, or Toby for that matter. We continued to find coveys and Pa continued to kill his usual two birds. I, on the other hand, started to miss more that I hit and Lemon had begun to give me that soulful look of sheer pity and contempt that a bird dog reserves for those who fail to do their part. It's damn embarrassing to be chastised by a dog and this only added to my shooting problems.

The sleet had turned to a mixture of snow and rain as the sky became a dark veil of black tumbling clouds. It was getting too dark to shoot so Pa decided to call it a day. Toby whistled up Lemon, who seemed relieved and ready to get back into his warm dog carrier. Lemon was not a fanatic. He liked to hunt, but he had been around long enough to appreciate life's small pleasures. The pointers would have wanted to hunt through the next ice age.

I broke open my shotgun to remove the shells. I made a point of showing Pa my empty gun before I placed it back in the fur lined gun case. I knew it made him feel better to just be sure. Toby counted our bag for the day and announced that we had nineteen birds, a little shy of our limit, but not bad for an easy walking hunt with an old setter.

We dropped Toby and the birds off at his house. He would clean and pick them before bringing half of them over to our house later that evening, in time for us to have them for supper. He and his family would keep the other half. As Toby left and went into his house, I asked Pa if he would be staying on after next Saturday's turnover?

"Yes, indeed," he replied. "Toby's one of my best hands, not to mention the best dog handler I know."

"Who else we gonna keep?"

"Well, you know I'm going to keep Crip and Tracey, they have been with me forever. They live in town and won't be affected by the change at all. I want Junior, Catfish and Little Man to stay as well. Junior and Catfish don't have a family and Little Man and Bessie don't have children. I plan to completely remodel five of the better houses. I'm gonna add running water, a septic system and electricity. There is no reason my hands should live like it was 1850."

"What about the families that will be leaving, where will they go?"

"I've talked to all twenty of them, and most want to stay in the Delta and keep on sharecropping. Three families wanted to go up

North, and I have agreed to pay for their transportation and give them a little money to get started."

"Who will get the ones who stay?"

"I've arranged for three really good farmers who I know will treat them right to be here early next Saturday and take their pick. I expect they will take the whole bunch."

"What if the hands don't want to go with them, do they have to?"

"Of course not, after all they aren't slaves."

"Oh, I guess they aren't"

Now that I understood the plan it made more sense to me. I was having a hard time thinking that some real red neck like Mr. Kyle might get all our hands and treat them poorly. We rode the rest of the way home with the sleet and snow hammering away on the truck cab.

The next Saturday morning dawned without a cloud in the sky, a perfect bluebird winter day. The cold front that had come through while we were bird hunting had passed as is often the case in the deep south and the freezing snow and sleet had given way to daytime highs in the 40s.

We had an early breakfast and were just finishing when the first farmers arrived to pick up our hands, and just as Pa had predicted, the three early arrivals took all of the available workers. We led the trucks around the place and helped load up what little household effects each family owned. By noon all the families were gone, and Pa and I were sitting on the back of his pickup talking to our remaining hands.

Crip, who by dent of his years of service and Pa's unspoken consent, was considered by all of the other hands to be the de facto farm foreman. As the last truck left our property and disappeared down the black top road, Crip said,

"Mistah, Rainer, there be anything else we need to do this mornin'?"

"No, Crip, I expect you can let everyone off for the afternoon. Toby and I have a couple of chores left to do, but we'll get to them later today."

"Yes suh, then I 'spect we'll be goin' back to town."

"Oh, there is one more thing I need to do." Pa said, as he reached inside the pickup and pulled out a bank deposit bag.

He unzipped the bag and took out five envelopes, one for each of the remaining hands.

"I have a little something to help y'all make the adjustment to our new system. I gave the families that just left us a little gift to help them get settled and as y'all know, I helped Leroy, Joe and Luther with their trip to Chicago. I felt that it was only fair that y'all who will be staying and making this place go should get a share as well."

He handed each of them an envelope with their names printed on them. I could tell that they had not been expecting anything like this and didn't know what to say.

Finally, Crip spoke for them all.

"Mistah Rainer, we surely thank you for this. All of us can really use it and so can our families. Thank you suh!"

"Glad to do it; I'll be counting on all of y'all to help me make this new system work."

"Yas Suh, you can shore count on us."

- "Well, y'all get out of here and don't let me see you till next Monday morning. Toby, take the truck home for dinner and come back over here about 2:30 and we'll go tend to that other business."

Everybody went on their way as Pa and I walked back to the house to wash up for dinner. My grandmother usually made a lighter dinner at noon on Saturday then she did on a regular work day. Today we had fried pork chops, mashed potatoes with brown gravy, collard greens and cornbread. After dinner Pa and I took a nap for about an hour and got up around 2:00pm. We had a big slice of lemon orange pound cake and a cup of coffee. We were ready to meet Toby and finish the day's work.

It wasn't long before Toby drove up with a dozen five- gallon gas cans in the back of the truck. I got in the middle and we drove off down the black top. We turned on a gravel road that led up to one of the recently vacated sharecropper houses, and pulled to a stop at the edge of the yard. Toby and Pa got out and each hefted one of the gas cans out of the truck bed.

They went in the front door of the little gray house and began to splash diesel fuel all over the floor and walls. They went to each room, and then circled the outside splashing diesel under each side of the house. When they had finished, Pa took a kitchen match and struck it on the box before lighting a handful of dry grass. He pitched the burning grass into the pool of diesel fuel on the front porch, and soon the whole house was crackling and burning with a long plume of dirty gray smoke curling into the winter sky.

Since the house was isolated in a patch of grass surrounded by turned-under cotton fields there was no chance of the blaze spreading. We pulled back on the gravel road and the inferno slipped away in our rearview mirror. We repeated this nineteen more times and by 4:00 we were back at the farm center.

The blue sky was filled with the black and gray plumes of smoke while the distinct smell of burning dwellings hung heavy on the breeze. We had dropped Toby off at his house and were again perched on the tailgate of Pa's truck looking at the pillars of smoke.

Pa looked over at me and said,

"In 54 BC the Romans invaded Britain. Julius Caesar led the Roman army and they made an unopposed landing on the channel coast. Legend has it that during that first night ashore, Caesar ordered the Roman boats be set on fire and destroyed. The logic was that in the morning, when the Legionnaires saw that there was no way to retreat, they would realize that they had no choice but to beat the defending Britons."

"Burned his boats? That meant that they were stuck there."

"Look out across these fields and you'll see our boats burning on the beach. We're stuck with running this place as a mechanized farm. We have no choice but to succeed."

For the next sixteen years, Pa was the most productive farmer in terms of pounds of lint per acre in Sunflower County and had the lowest cost per pound of cotton. The smell of his burning boats lingered for years to come.

Royal Ambassadors

It was full daylight when I woke up. I could tell that no one else was awake because the attic fan still pulled the cool morning air across my bed. This artificial breeze brought with it the faint smell of yesterday's newly mown grass mixed with the rich aroma of Confederate Jasmine and Sweet Olives. There was just the hint of cotton poison and a touch of last night's DDT truck blending into the overall effect. Summer in the Mississippi Delta.

As much as I wanted to lie there and soak up the cool fragrances' of morning, I had to get up and get going. Today was Saturday and there was baseball to be played. I slid out of bed and reached for a rumpled pair of jeans and slipped them on. Socks and tennis shoes followed, the whole thing was topped by a faded Mississippi State tee-shirt and Bulldog baseball cap. I was fully outfitted for a day at the diamond.

I grabbed my Peewee Reese fielder's glove, my Ted Williams Louisville Slugger and tiptoed to the kitchen. I opened the refrigerator and grabbed a bottle of milk. I took several big swigs of the ice cold milk, straight from the bottle. I immediately felt a twinge of guilt. My mother didn't have many hard fast rules, but "don't drink from the milk bottle" along with "always wear clean underwear" were chief among them. This morning I was violating both taboos.

Oh well, what she doesn't know can't hurt her, or more importantly, can't hurt me.

She'd probably know I did it, along with not changing underwear, as soon as she got up. I didn't know how she'd know, but I suspected she had hidden cameras strategically placed throughout the house. Maybe she was just way ahead of her time on DNA testing. Dad and I never knew, but we suspected that she might be a psychic, or possibly, a witch.

I overcame my little twinge of guilt, grabbed a banana and slipped out the kitchen door. I found my bike propped on the side of the open carport. I stuck the bat and glove in my basket, peeled my banana back and headed toward the ballpark.

Little League Baseball started in Williamsport, Pa. in 1939. By 1953 it had pretty much spread across the nation, but it had not penetrated the Mississippi Delta. There were probably several good reasons for this, but I have always suspected that it was tainted by the specter of being a Yankee invention. Anything so cursed would be suspect in a society that refused to celebrate the 4th of July because of the fall of Vicksburg in 1863.

We might not have had Little League, but we actually had something much better. Our baseball was tribal based and was governed by hard and fast customs and rules. There were no inept adult coaches and umpires; these roles were filled by the older guys, who for the most part, were top-quality ball players. The adults in our little world played softball for the Volunteer Fire Department, and were a hell of lot more concerned with BBQ and beer than our athletic development.

I stopped by Benny's house on my way to the park. He was sitting in his driveway, drinking his usual nutritious breakfast of a bottle of Coke. He mounted his bike and we rode the five blocks to the Cumberland City Park, the site of today's baseball game. Our version of baseball was divided into two distinct groups. The A league, in which the older guys, say from 15 to 18, played, and the B league for the rest of us. Both groups played at City Park and both games were all day affairs, starting about 8:00 am on Saturday morning and lasting till it was too dark to see. The A league played on the Volunteer Fire Department's softball field which had lights and dugouts. The rest of us played on a much more modest diamond that barely had bases and a pitcher's mound.

Both leagues organized the Saturday games the same way. The players gathered early in the morning, two captains were voted on, and the captains took turns choosing their players from the available talent pool. Those players not chosen in the first round stayed on the sidelines until one of the starters got hurt, had to go home or just wanted a break. Then the team captain would pick a replacement from the sideline pool. In the course of the day everyone would, sooner or later, get a chance to play. The only way you could advance from the B league to the A was by being invited. Talent ruled the day and good friends might be in different leagues.

Benny and I were regular starters in the B league, but we didn't want to be late for the choosing. That could mean sitting on the sidelines for several hours waiting for an opening. In addition to leaving the game for voluntary reasons, you were automatically benched if you made an error or pulled some stupid stunt like a balk or a base-running mistake. The system was brutal and there was no appeal. If you wanted to play, you had best learn the game. There was none of that "every kid gets to play" Kum ba ya that Dads, whose sons couldn't chew gum and walk at the same time, invented.

There were about a dozen guys hanging around the B ball field and we knew them all. Some were regular starters and others were wannabe's. A couple of kids were as young as nine or ten. We parked our bikes and trotted over to the crowd. Things would be getting started soon. Benny was usually elected as one of the captains. He played a mean shortstop and was a consistent hitter.

I ,on the other hand , was all hit, no field. I had learned to be a switch hitter by playing on an undersized lot when I visited my Pensacola grandparents. You had to bat opposite your natural swing in order to keep the ball out of Palafox Highway. I was probably the best hitter in the B league, which would all change the first time I saw a high school curve ball, but for now I was the Sultan of Swat.

The fact that I was a little iffy in the fielding department, and could barely throw the ball back to the infield from my permanent perch in right field, kept me from being a really hot property. I would never be elected one of the captains, but I would always get picked in the first bunch. Benny would pick me up if I lasted for four or five rounds, but only after he got his pitcher and infielders. Benny loved defense and I wasn't much of a defensive asset. He just stuck me in right field and hoped no one hit anything my way. I rarely made an error, but anything hit deep to right was going for extra bases.

We were just about to start the election of captains when a battered pickup truck pulled all up on the grass and headed our way. Stan Rushing, the youth director of the First Baptist Church stepped out and signaled for us to gather around him.

"Hi guys," he started, "I'm Stan Rushing, Youth Minister at First Baptist. I have an announcement and some flyers to pass around."

He started handing out mimeographed sheets and continued,

"First Baptist is forming a Royal Ambassador's youth baseball team that will compete in the Delta Baptist Convention League. There will be twelve teams in the league representing most of the towns in the Delta. I will be coach of the team and I will be holding tryouts Sunday afternoon. I am hoping to see all of y'all at the tryouts. You must be at least eleven years old as of June 1 and no more than fourteen. I will pick a traveling squad of twenty-five. Two guys at each position, four pitchers and three managers. Do any of you have questions?

"I do," I said, "I'm an Episcopalian, will I be able to try out?"

"Absolutely, your denomination won't matter, just your baseball skills. The only requirement is that you will have to join our Chapter of the Royal Ambassadors. There is one other little catch: in order to be in the Royal Ambassadors, you will have to attend Sunday school and church with us each Sunday. Other than that, anyone is welcome."

Oh, that's all there is to it, huh? I'll have to really work to finesse this by the goalie at home.

Rushing fielded a few more questions and was soon back in his truck and at work in the local vineyards of sinners. The news had caused quite a stir and everyone was talking about it.

"Well, what do you think about that?" I asked Benny.

"Maybe a good deal. Rushing played baseball and ran track at Mississippi College. He probably knows what he's doing."

"Yeah, from the little I know about him, he seems to be a straight arrow, but a pretty nice guy. We'll have to clean up our language if we do this."

"Oh, what the hell, that shouldn't be a problem," Benny said with one of his big grins.

"Yeah, that's what I'm afraid of. I'm going to take the flyer home and run it up the flagpole to see if anybody salutes it."

"I'm sure I can do it," Benny said, "Hell, they hardly ever know what I doing anyway, and I know Sunday morning won't be a problem. Dad will be teeing off at the Club and Mom will still be asleep till after Church."

"I may run into a little more resistance," I said, "It will all depend on Mom's current religious affiliations. I may be able to catch her between conversions, who knows?"

We spent the rest of Saturday playing baseball, and by the time we headed home, the stars were peeking out. I parked my bike by the back door and eased into the kitchen. We usually had sandwiches on Saturday evening. I would have been out doing something all day, while Dad would have been playing gin at the VFW or American Legion clubs. Tonight would be no exception; there was no visible kitchen action.

Dad was sitting in his chair watching the end of a Yankee-Red Sox game, eating a sandwich and drinking a beer. He looked up and said,"Hi, how'd you play today?"

"About usual, I got a bunch of hits and didn't embarrass myself in the field. There is something I need to talk to you about."

"Am I going to like this?"

"I hope so," I said, handing him the flyer about the new league.

He read it over and said, "Looks like a good idea to me. Think you can make the team?"

"Probably, but I might need your help getting it by you-know-who. This has religious overtones which means she'll be all over it."

"Whoa, Bubba, you're not going to drag me into that swamp. I don't discuss religion with your mother."

"I'll handle the negotiations; just back me up when she comes to you for the tie-breaking vote. By the way, do you know the brand she is currently into?"

"Last I heard she was a Christian Scientist, but that was a couple of months ago. Today, who knows?"

He turned back to the ballgame signaling the end to our little moment of quality time together. I began to formulate my strategy concerning my mother. She was a kind, caring person, but when it came to religion she was a complete nut case. She had been raised as a Southern Baptist and married my Dad, who had been raised a Catholic, and had attended Jesuit schools. As soon as he left home, he vowed that he would never darken the door of another church of any ilk.

When I was born, my grandmother on my Dad's side had me christened in the Episcopal Church because she had been raised an Episcopalian before converting to The Church of Rome when she married. During World War II, I lived with my maternal grandmother, who was a Christian Scientist. I attended Sunday School at the First Baptist Church, but only because my grandmother's best friend was the pastor's wife.

When the war ended in 1945 my parents returned to Mississippi and I was pretty much stuck with whatever my mother was into. We had brief encounters with most of the mainstream Protestant sects and some of the less extreme evangelical groups. There was a brief encounter with the Greek Orthodox Church when mother bought a cook book. She spent a couple of years as a Roman Catholic during which she did her best to convert my agnostic father back to the true church.

He considered all forms of organized religion to be scams designed to manipulate the masses, and besides he liked to play gin on Sunday mornings. He escaped her clutches, but I was always forced to go along with the faith de jour. I had managed to avoid any formal rites of conversion in all but the Catholic Church. She had me baptized before she decided to move on.

When I reached the age of reason, in this case about ten years old, I put my foot down and announced that hence forth I would be attending the Episcopal Church, thank you very much. The young priest at Cumberland's Church of The Holy Trinity listened to my story, checked it out with my Dad (Mother would not talk to him), and at last my spiritual journey was at an end, or so I thought.

Tonight I would have to appear before mother's ecclesiastical court and plead my case for a brief detour from my Anglican path in order to play baseball. I did not expect her to be sympathetic to my plan. She didn't want me to be an Episcopalian, but if I insisted on it, she would want me to be faithful to my creed. Attendance at First Baptist would not please her.

I waited until I had finished my sandwich and caught her in the kitchen puttering about. I brought the flyer with me. I carefully chose my moment and said,

"Mom, do you have a minute? I want to share something with you."

She turned and looked at me with suspicion and a little apprehension.

"What are you up to now?" She asked.

"Gee, Mom, do I have to be up to something?"

"You may not be aware of it, but the only time you ever initiate a conversation with me is when you want something, and it's usually something that I disagree with."

Hmm, she might have a point there. My basic policy is to have as little direct contact with authority as possible, thus reducing the opportunity for advice and instructions. I might have to adjust this to include an occasional casual conversation without a motive. Something to consider.

"Well, this time it is something that I believe you can relate to. I have decided to broaden my spiritual horizons and spend the summer examining other religions. I don't intend to abandon the Episcopal Church, but I think I should learn about other faiths."

"I'll have to admit that you have surprised me with this attitude, and I am certainly pleased that you are open minded enough to examine other beliefs. What do you have in mind?"

"I thought that I would first have a conversation with Father Mullen at Holy Trinity, to enlist his guidance and support, then I might start my quest at First Baptist."

"You know how I feel about that, but I suppose you need to make up your own mind. I can't see any real harm in giving it a try, just don't get consumed by the hellfire and brimstone."

Actually, I had no idea how she felt about First Baptist or Shintoism for that matter, but I recognized all of the "buy signals" and decided to close the sale before I talked her out of it."

"I'm glad you approve, you know I respect your views on religion. I'll get everything cleared with Father Mullen next week and start to visit First Baptist next Sunday."

"I want you to keep me up to date as you move along your pilgrimage, I might have some suggestions on where you should go next, there is a very interesting new pastor at the Church of God in Boyle. You might want to check them out."

"Yes ma'am, I'll keep that in mind."

Who knows? The Church of God could have a Lacrosse team, I've always wanted to try Lacrosse.

Later, I overheard my mother relating our conversation to my father, who to his credit, grunted in the right places and didn't blow my cover. He came into my room before he went to bed and said.

"That was skillfully done. I want to award you both ears and the tail."

"What in the world are you talking about, both ears and the tail?"

"Look it up. Again, well done!"

"Will you sign the parental permission form?"

"Sure, give it to me."

I was on my way to tomorrow's tryouts.

I was scheduled to be the acolyte at the early morning prayer service the next day and I cornered Father Mullen in his office studying the collects and lessons for the day. I stuck my head in and said, "Good morning, Father, do you have a moment to spare me?"

He set aside his cup of coffee and invited me to have a seat.

"What can I do for you, Tommy?' He asked.

I explained my plan in detail and asked for his permission to carry it out.

"I really can't see any real harm in what you plan to do. I realize that the quest for spiritual information is really a ruse to get it by your mother, and knowing your mother, I think it is the only chance you had to get her to buy into the deal. I'd rather debate Satan himself than to have a conversation on comparative religions with Kathleen Larch."

"I figure I could make the seven o'clock morning prayer service and still have time to be at First Baptist at nine for Sunday school and church. I don't think I'll be required to attend the Sunday night service so I can still make it to EYC."

"That's a lot of religion just to play baseball. I hope you can pull it off."

"I guess you'll just have to have a little faith."

Sunday dinner was the big deal meal of the week and attendance was mandatory. No one ever had to urge my participation, the fried chicken alone assured that I would be there and ready to pig out. My mother was a good cook and she had all of her mother's recipes.

My grandmother was to country cooking what Ted Williams was to hitting a baseball. Dead on the best there was.

The mandatory aspects of the meal were really aimed at my gin-playing father, he had been known to lose track of time at the card table and miss the whole deal. He would just as soon have a plate warmed up about three o'clock, but it would send my mother into orbit. She would be angry for a week and everybody's life would be miserable. I always called the club about thirty minutes before we were to sit down and remind him to come home. This usually worked. He didn't like conflict or confrontation and my mother was the drama queen of the Delta. She thrived on recreational confrontation.

Dad showed up on time and the meal went off without a hitch. I helped clear the table and dried the dishes. I made inane small talk as part of my new "mother manipulation" program. I had to be sure to use a very light touch; it could be very dangerous to manipulate the master manipulator. I was trying to beard the lion in her den and it would be very easy to screw it up. I managed to make it through the cleanup and eased over into nap time.

Every Sunday afternoon my parents took a nap after dinner. My little brother was forced to participate, but I was allowed to skip the nap time, if I got out of the house. This suited me fine and as everyone retired to their rooms, I headed to the ballpark for tryouts. I biked to Benny's house and gently knocked on the back door. Benny came out, admonishing me to be quiet.

"She went back to bed when he left to go play golf. I got him to sign the permission slip as he left. He didn't even read it. You get yours signed?"

"Yeah, it required some doing, but I have it."

"Now we have to make the team. It would be a bitch to have to watch them play from the stands."

When we got to the park there were about twenty guys standing around and no sign of Rushing. Another dozen or so candidates drifted in before the old battered pickup rolled up. Coach Rushing dismounted and motioned for everyone to gather around him and take a knee.

"I'm glad to see all of y'all. Now we are going to move right along and choose our team. Does everybody have their permission forms signed?"

This was met with a chorus of, "*Yeah, Coach.*"

"Good, pass them up to Benny; he is going to be my assistant this afternoon."

This was a positive start. I doubted that Rushing would make Benny his assistant if he didn't plan to pick him for the team.

"Here's how we are gonna do this thing. First, we are going to check out everyone's speed and quickness. Let's line up on the first base line and we'll sprint to the fence in left field and back."

Let me say right away that speed and quickness were not my long suits. I just needed to finish in the top twenty or so. It's like the two hikers being chased by a grizzly bear; you don't have to out run the bear, just your fellow hiker.

Following the sprints, we went through the usual fielding drills with Rushing hitting fungos to each of the guys. Benny and I were pretty good fielders, and we passed this test with ease. Fortunately, Rushing did not ask us to demonstrate our long throwing ability and I slid by unnoticed. When the tryouts ended, Coach Rushing said that the final roster would be announced at the next meeting of the Royal Ambassadors after school on Wednesday. He got in his truck and left. A couple of guys wanted to get a game up, but Benny and I decided to bike over to the Keen Freeze and get a coke. I wanted to make sure that whatever took place at my house on Sunday afternoons had plenty of time to reach a climax. A couple of hours should be plenty.

The new baseball team was the hot topic the next week at school. Everyone who had tried out showed signs of anticipation and anxiety. I was sure Benny had made the team, and I really thought that I had, but you never know when adults are in charge.

They tend to make some really strange decisions. Finally, on Wednesday afternoon Benny and I rode our bikes straight to First Baptist and the Royal Ambassador's meeting.

We parked at a bike rack just outside the door to a building with a sign proclaiming "Fellowship Hall". The whole complex was much different than it had been during my Sunbeam days, and nothing looked familiar. We were trying to figure our next move when we saw Coach Rushing walking across the parking lot. He waved and said,

"Hi guys, we're going to meet in one of the large Sunday school classrooms. Give me a minute to drop by my office and I'll let y'all in."

"Thanks, Coach" we replied as we noticed several other guys looking just as confused as we were.

"Hey, y'all come over here, Coach has gone to get the keys to our meeting room, and he'll be right back."

By the time Rushing returned pretty much the whole contingent of hopeful players was on hand, plus some guys who must have been non-ball playing members of the Royal Ambassadors. He led us into the Fellowship Hall and opened the door to what appeared to be your standard school class room. There were large windows facing the outside of the building, chalk boards in front, bookshelves on the third wall and a storage room in the back

There were religious posters all over the place, most depicting scenes from the Bible and some showing missionaries at work in pagan lands such as Mexico and Canada. Coach asked everyone to find a seat and turned the meeting over to Larry Bemis, the current president of the club. Larry stood up and said,

"Let's all bow our heads and open our meeting with a moment of silence followed by the Lord's Prayer."

Once the prayer was out of the way, there were some opening ceremonies to be observed and the meeting was called to order. We then sang a ragged rendition of Onward Christian Soldiers and someone read the Royal Ambassador's creed. Larry then read a Bible verse dealing with the parable of the Good Samaritan, and we were all invited to comment on what we thought the parable meant. After a lengthy discussion with no real consensus, Larry announced that next week's Bible reading would be about the wedding in Cana. So far no mention of baseball.

Finally Larry suggested that we move on to the business portion of our meeting and asked for a report on the RA Project. Another kid that I didn't know reported that the RA mothers' cake sale had netted $23.89 and that amount had been sent to the Chapter's mission church in Kenya. Still no baseball.

At long last, Larry suggested that Rev. Rushing had an announcement concerning the RA baseball team.

Coach Rushing stood and said,

"I have posted the final roster for our new baseball team on the bulletin board in the hall. I suggest that each of you who tried out for the team consult the roster as soon as the meeting ends. For those of you who have been selected, our first practice will be at the Volunteer Fire Department's main field at 3:00 pm tomorrow. Now Larry you may close the meeting in the usual manner."

Two prayers and one hymn later, having found our names on the roster, we were back in the parking lot getting our bikes.

The team had a couple of weeks to practice before the season started, and by the time we played our first game, we had put together a pretty good ball club. Coach Rushing knew the game and he coached with a light, but firm hand. Our games were after school on Tuesday and Thursday which left us time for our regular Saturday pickup games at the park.

By the time school ended in early June, we were about half-way through our schedule with a record of 8 wins and 4 losses. Not the best in the league, but far from the worst. If we could keep it up, we'd make the playoffs for sure. The winner of the Delta League would go to Nashville and play in the Royal Ambassadors World Series. We were in the hunt. Benny and I faithfully attended the RA meetings, Sunday school and Church. Everything was going along just fine.

It was the last Sunday in June. I got up early and did my acolyte duty at Holy Trinity and steered my bike toward First Baptist. The full heat of the Delta summer would not come until the end of July or the first of August, but today was probably the warmest so far. I had plenty of time to ride the six or so blocks between churches and I tried to stay on the shady side of the street and take my time.

Sunday morning is generally a quiet time in most of rural America and this was a nearly perfect early summer day. The blue sky was accented by a few pure white clouds and the warm air smelled of morning glories and honeysuckle. The leafy residential streets of Cumberland were ruffled by a light breeze that felt good as I rode slowly along.

I parked my bike in the rack, went into the First Baptist fellowship hall and found our Sunday school classroom. Benny and John Tong, the catcher on our RA baseball team, were sitting waiting for class to begin.

"Hi, guys," I said, "What's up?"

"Nothin' much" John said, "How 'bout you?"

"Just plowing through my Sunday morning obligations, I've done the Episcopal thing and now its Baptist time."

After Sunday school there was a break before Church started and Benny, John and I decided to skip the punch and cookies and take a walk in the nice weather. We strolled around the block and managed to kill the thirty minutes before the main service started. The three of us dutifully filed into the main sanctuary and scored the last three aisle seats in a pew about half way to the front.

The service started with the choir singing The Old Rugged Cross. There was an opening prayer that was all encompassing and called God's attention to most everything and everybody. The church was filled almost to capacity, and with no air conditioning, became warm and stuffy. Soon the ushers were moving down both sides of the sanctuary opening the large windows and letting in the light summer breeze. Immediately the level of comfort improved considerably. The Pastor was reading the Old Testament Scripture for the day and as he finished the congregation broke into a spirited rendition of Glorious Things of Thee are Spoken which was followed by Wonderful, Merciful Savior.

I have to admit, I really enjoyed the old traditional hymns sung at First Baptist and to this day recall that part of my Baptist Summer with affection. When the last strains of the hymns died down the Pastor read the New Testament Scripture and the combination of beautiful music and the summer breeze had a soothing effect on the soul and body. When my soul and body were soothed, I tended to nap.

Following a rousing version of Rock of Ages, The Pastor launched into his sermon for the day. The three of us were attempting to look as attentive as possible as he assailed sin in all of its many forms. The gist of the message seemed to be that Satan would test each of us in many ways before we could enter God's glory. At about this point the soothing overtook the potential sinning and I lost touch with the here and now. The droning of the Pastors voice coupled with the warm, sweet scented air lulled me into my own thoughts and I became disconnected from my surroundings. I wasn't asleep, but darn close.

Suddenly the organ blasted away with the first bars of How Great is Our God and everyone in the congregation stood. John tapped me on the shoulder and whispered,

"Let's go."

I assumed that the service was over and John wanted to get a head start on our exit. The three of us, led by John, started moving out of our pew, but rather than turning left and heading toward the exit, John hung a right and started down the aisle toward the front of the Church. Like lemmings Benny and I followed behind him and the three of us walked slowly toward the Pastor who was standing at the pulpit with his eyes closed and his arms outstretched.

At this point my head began to clear a bit and I realized two horrifying facts. Church was not over; we were at the point known as The Invitation. It was now that anyone who wished to accept Jesus Christ as his personal Savior was invited to come on down. The second fact was that John Tong was in a state of spiritual rapture and heading for salvation. Benny and I had been scooped up in the net of John's new found fervor.

I desperately looked for an escape route. There was none. We were caught up in events beyond our control with no choice but to go with the flow. Now it became a matter of making the most out of a bad situation and saving face. When we reached the Pastor, he opened his eyes and a huge smile split his normally stern visage.

"Praise the Lord!" he shouted, "these three young men have been moved by the spirit to accept Jesus as their personal Savior. Praise the Lord!"

Two of the deacons came up and led us to the side door in the sanctuary and into a hall that led directly behind the pulpit. We entered a small dimly lit room that smelled just like the dressing rooms at the swimming pool. We came out of our church clothes and stripped to our skivvies. One of the attending deacons handed us a white jumper that looked like a nightshirt. We were then led to a room that held a large tank of water with steps leading into it. There was the Pastor who had changed clothes and now wore a set of black and white robes.

He descended the steps into the water which came up about to his chest and motioned for John to join him in the tank. The water came up almost to John's neck and the jumper kept floating revealing his skivvies. At that point, the heavy red curtain that stood behind the pulpit began to open and we were facing the entire congregation of the First Baptist Church of Cumberland. The front of the tank was made of glass and everyone had an aquarium view of John Tong's shorts.

The Pastor put his thumb and forefinger on John's nose and dipped him backwards into the tank until his head was underwater and said,

"John, I baptize you in the name of the Father, the Son and the Holy Ghost. Welcome into Christ's Church, John!"

Beaming with divine sanctification John ascended the stairs to dry land and I was invited to descend into the tank. After my baptism, Benny followed and soon we were all back in our church clothes and rejoining the congregation.

The service concluded with all six verses of A Closer Walk with Thee after which we were the center of congratulations and attention for about another twenty minutes. When the crowd began to drift away and head home for fried chicken or pot roast, we three new workers in the vineyards of righteousness found ourselves alone in the parking lot.

"Exactly how in the hell did that happen?" Benny asked, with some amount of irritation in his voice.

"Don't ask me," I said, "I was following Tong."

John, who seemed to be coming out of his advanced state of grace, looked a little puzzled and said,

"I'm not really sure what happened. One minute I was perfectly sane, and before I knew it I was swept away in the moment. All I can say is that it seemed like a good idea at the time."

"I guess it will be all over town within the hour." Benny mused, "I better get home and prepare them before my aunt has a chance to call." He grabbed his bike and quickly pedaled out of sight.

"Yeah, this poses a couple of possible problems for me too, not the least of which is that this was my third baptism. I hope that the three of them don't cancel each other out or something."

John had not said another word but was standing there with a stricken look on his face.

"You okay?" I asked.

"Not really," he said, "I've got to go explain this to my Buddhist parents. This will probably disturb the karma of some seventy generations of my ancestors or at least my mother will say it does."

In the end, John decided that it would be best if he didn't mention his conversion to his parents. He rationalized that since they didn't speak very good English, it would only confuse them. This also assured that he would be able to continue playing on the RA team.

Benny's parents didn't seem particularly interested in his new found faith and pretty much left it with an *"Isn't that nice?"* comment. His aunt never mentioned it.

I checked the whole thing out with Father Mullen and he allowed that it would not affect my status in the Episcopal Church , and what the heck, it couldn't hurt my spiritual condition. My mother wanted to know all about it and seemed fascinated. I was afraid she would show up at First Baptist some Sunday morning ready to take a dip. Dad just rolled his eyes and muttered something about religious fanatics. Things returned to normal and we made the playoffs, but got beat before we got to Nashville.

Coach Rushing declared the season a huge success and said that he looked forward to next year. Before we knew it football season was underway and my adventure in the Royal Ambassadors drew to a close.

August 15th

The alarm clock sounded at 6:30 and I reached to my window sill to turn it off. Though it was only 6:30, I had been awake since dawn, my mind racing with anticipation. Today was August 15th. The first day of football practice.

Two years before, Cumberland High had fielded a Delta Valley Conference Championship team – 10-0, undefeated and nearly unchallenged. The Championship team only had 31 players total, and the starting eleven were all seniors. Most were now playing college football on some level. One in the SEC, a couple more at smaller four year schools, and the rest at two-year junior colleges.

Last year we were 0-10 and lost to Carney High School, which is about a third the size of Cumberland and A to our AAA. The entire town was humiliated and the coaching staff held a special assembly program urging any decent athlete to try out when fall practice started. Bodies were needed.

There were five of us who would be starting the eighth grade in September, and we decided to take up the call for players. Benny and I worked out every afternoon all summer, with the exception of the two weeks we spent at Fort McClellan with Company D of the 155th Infantry, Mississippi National Guard. Those two weeks were very physical, and we lost no edge. If anything, we came back tougher than we left, which I suppose was what the Army had in mind to start with.

I rolled out of bed, put on my underwear, shorts and a tee shirt. I thought I'd better wear my tennis shoes just in case. I stopped by the refrigerator, and took a long swig from a bottle of milk, then hit the back door. It wasn't even seven o'clock and the heat slammed into me like an open oven, the ever-present smell of boll weevil poison and mosquito spray floating in the damp morning air. The aerial application of pesticides was a daily thing.

The Mississippi Delta in mid August is no place for sissies. We were lucky if it got below 85 °F at night. Today was supposed to be a scorcher, over 100 °F with suffocating moisture in the heavy air, a perfect start for "two-a-days".

I hopped on my bike and headed to Benny's house,. By the time I managed the three-block ride I was sweating like a field hand. Benny was sitting on his bike waiting for me. We headed for the gym and whatever fate awaited us.

We rode up to the gym as about fifty other guys got there on bikes, in cars, pickup trucks and on foot. Everyone was milling around trying to find their friends, and soon the five eighth-graders had formed a little knot in the back of the room. We were looking at the older guys with some degree of apprehension when a shrill whistle interrupted the clamor.

Coach W.R. "Rig" Wiley stood loosely at ease. He was a fireplug of a man standing about 5' 8" tall and about 5' thick. He had been a drill sergeant, a gunnery sergeant, combat veteran of both the Pacific and Korea, and by the way, had been welter weight champion of the entire USMC. His hair was cut short in the military manner, his arms rippled with all sorts of muscles, tendons, veins and God only knows what else. His body was covered with wire-like sandy colored hair and his freshly shaven square jaw had already begun to show a new crop of stubble. He looked like a recruiting poster for the Marine Corp. This made sense: He had everyone's rapt attention.

"Okay, girls, I'm not going to say this but once, so listen up. We're going to divide into two groups. Everyone who was on last year's team go to my right, everyone else go to my left. Both groups form a single file and keep your damn mouth shut. I'll take the returning players with me to the locker room and Coach Biles will take you rookies."

There was not a sound in the gym as Coach Wiley and his charges left for the locker room. Coach Biles strolled over to us.

"Anyone who has ever played football on any level raise your hand," he growled.

About half of the group, including the five Eighth-graders, raised their hands and he added,

"I want these guys to go to the other end of the gym with Coach Kemp and the rest of you stay with me. All right , let's move out."

By now our group had been reduced to about fifteen and we followed Coach Kemp to the back of the gym.

"I'm John Kemp and I will be coaching the B team this year. I played fullback and linebacker at Delta State for the past two years, and I will be teaching chemistry this year. I don't know many of you, but I do recognize Bowman and Larch sitting in the back of the group. I'm a platoon sergeant in "D" Company of the 155th Infantry and they are two of my troopers."

We were stunned; this was the first time he had ever shown any indication that we existed. We were petrified. He looked at us and said,

"You guys enjoy summer training this year?"

"Yes, sergeant!" we shouted in unison.

"Well that's good to hear, this is gonna be a hell of a lot worse. Here's the deal. I am going to pass out these consent forms for your parents to sign. Bring them back by the start of practice tomorrow morning. If you lose the form and don't have it here in the morning, I suggest that you bend over, stick your head between your legs and kiss your ass goodbye. Your soul may belong to God, but your ass is mine. AM I CLEAR?"

"Yes, Sergeant!" the two of us screamed. Everyone else just looked shell shocked.

Stifling a grin, Coach Kemp looked at us and said,

"'Coach', will do around here guys, but I like your enthusiasm. Next we're going to move to the girl's gym and you maggots are going to get a physical to separate the quick and the soon to wish they were dead."

We filed silently across the covered walkway separating the boys' gym from the girls'. The contrast was immediately clear. The boys' gym floor had not been refinished in years; it was covered with scuff marks and black streaks. The bleachers were run down and the whole thing looked ratty. Cumberland prided itself as a football school. The boys' basketball team usually sucked. The girls' gym was pristine: freshly refinished floor with a new coat of varnish, and new bleachers that would seat twice as many fans as the male version.

Benny and I had never set foot in this sanctuary of female privilege. John Kemp was about to find out why.

Coach Kemp led us across the gym floor heading for the other end where "Doc" Fitzgerald had set up his scales and other equipment. We made it about ten feet when the door to Coach Peggy Wood's office burst open and a deep gravelly voice rang out,

"Hey dumbass. what the hell do you think you're doing?"

Coach Kemp stopped abruptly and said, "Are you talking to me?"

"Do you see another dumbass marching half of the brats in Sunflower County across my freshly painted gym floor?" She fumed.

"Well to start with, I didn't realize you owned the gym, and secondly, Coach Wiley gave us permission to be here."

Peggy Woods marched up to Coach Kemp and looked him directly in the eye. Kemp was 6'3" and, so was Peggy. Kemp probably weighed in at about 220 pounds. Peggy had him by an additional twenty or so. She was a formidable woman. She had been an All American basketball player at Delta State in the late thirties and her record as head coach at Cumberland High was 548 - 61. She had won thirteen Delta Valley Championships and six State titles. Nobody, and I mean nobody, screwed around with Peggy Woods. Coach Kemp was about to learn this the hard way.

Coach Woods started chewing his ass out in her best drill sergeant voice. She used words and expletives that exceeded anything I had heard at Fort McClellan. As she shouted, she began to chest bump him like a baseball manager does an umpire. Coach

Kemp was steady retreating. Finally she took a breath and he began apologizing as quickly as he could. Before she could get cranked up again, he led us back out the door we had just come in.

As we scuttled out of Coach Wood's fiefdom, we heard her parting shot to the doctor that had been waiting on us,

"Andy Fitzgerald, you get all of your crap together and get out of my gym. You can poke and prod that group of losers in the damn parking lot for all I care. Just get out of my gym."

By the time she finished screaming, Doctor Fitzgerald had followed us back to the boys' gym.

Coach Kemp and Doctor Fitzgerald were badly shaken. There was not much that could rattle John Kemp, but he had just met a force of nature too big to handle. We reorganized, completed the physicals, and were ordered to proceed to the locker room where we would be issued practice gear and attend a team meeting. The managers had filled the returning player's lockers with a complete set of brand new equipment: pads, pants, practice jerseys, shoes, tee shirts, socks and jocks. They even had new Riddell helmets.

We were assigned the leftover lockers. Benny and I would be sharing one of the old ones that didn't have a door. The managers came by each rookie's locker and started handing out the used equipment leftover from the last forty years. Benny and I got shoes that were cracked and missing cleats, pads that had pieces missing, pants that were permanently grass stained, jerseys that had been washed to near transparency and Jim Thorpe helmets. We did get new socks and jocks.

Coach Wiley blew his whistle, and we all fell quiet.

"Before we get dressed and start our first practice there is one more little item to attend to. The managers are going to assign a rookie to each of the returning letterman. When you find out who you've been assigned to, find him and he'll give you the drill on being a rookie. Now get dressed and be on the practice field in ten minutes."

The managers handed each of us a piece of paper. I looked at mine and it read "Jesse Carr".

I looked at Benny and said, "Does this remind you of Fort McClellan? I just got assigned to be Jesse Carr's rookie."

Jesse was a corporal in our Guard unit and an infantry platoon squad leader.

"You bet your ass it does, except the Army did give us new equipment and a locker with doors."

By the time we got our gear on we looked a lot like a 1920's version of a football player. The helmets were so old that they didn't have a chin strap; you tied it with a shoe lace. Norman Rockwell would have loved us.

One of the managers came by and said, "Show me the bottom of your shoes."

I complied and he handed me a handful of aluminum cleats.

"Before you go out there, be sure you have a tight cleat on every post. Somebody could get hurt if you don't. I don't want to have to take them in for stitches. Plus, they'd probably beat your ass for being stupid."

I noticed right away that the managers did not treat us with the same deference shown to the varsity players. There was just so much shit I was willing to take from the little snarfs and promised myself that a conversation on the school grounds might be in order. Benny and I ran across the parking lot to the practice field and the shit hit the fan. As soon as we hit the cinder track Coach Kemp met us with a scream.

"Give me four laps around the field and don't trot, run! Hey, Bowman, I mean the whole field, track, stadium and practice field. Run the fence."

By this time, it was 10:30 am and the sun was blasting down with a vengeance. The heat was rising from the freshly mown grass along with the sweet aroma of summer. It was like running through a field of hot oatmeal. Now there are several gaits that seemed to be acceptable starting with a dead-out run. I was certain that I could not make the four laps around the entire athletic complex at a run, so we were going to have to choose a slower, but acceptable, pace. I picked a jog, just a little faster than double time, but still slower than a run. Benny fell in beside me looking completely comfortable. Running had never bothered him and he could go forever. At Fort McClellan, we had run three miles every morning with full combat gear including our personal weapons, and it had been just as hot. The football gear rattled and shook, but so had the steel helmet and web equipment at McClellan. At least we didn't have an M-1 rifle to worry with.

Before we completed the first lap we began to pass some of the new guys that had started before us. By the end of the second lap we noticed several guys lying down in the grass puking up their breakfast and by the middle of the third lap we began to pass some of the varsity players who looked like they might be dying soon. When we huffed and puffed to the end of the fourth lap we realized that we had finished in the top fifteen. Those that remained were dragging, staggering and stumbling.

Coach Kemp told our group of finishers to get down on one knee and take a break while we waited on the rest of the guys to finish. The managers went to the aid of the staggering and sick, and eventually they all stumbled across the finish. While managers provided help and encouragement, they did not offer water or shade. Puffy white clouds were scattered in a deep blue sky. I picked up some of the mown grass and dropped it to see the direction of the breeze. There was no breeze and the day got hotter. I tried to spit but I had cotton mouth. All I could come up with were little puffs of white foam.

Coach Wiley's whistle blew again and we were told to rally around him and take a knee.

"That was pitiful," he said in a calm voice.

"Fifteen out of fifty managed to finish with some semblance of order. The rest of you are stragglers. This afternoon when we start

71

practice we are going to do it again, and we are going to do it right. The coaches and managers will run with you and no man will be allowed to straggle. Each of you will be responsible for helping a teammate in distress. Everyone will finish and everyone will be together. Am I clear?"

I looked at Benny and said, "Did you get that?"

"You mean the part about doing it all over again this afternoon, Yeah, I got it."

"At least we finished," I said, "That's something."

"It got us a five-minute break, but I missed the part where they passed out the water."

"I got a feeling water is gonna be a little scarce out here."

The whistle blew again and we began doing basic exercises with the coaches leading. I hadn't noticed until now that I was completely drenched in sweat. My jock was soaked, my shoulder pads were soggy and my shoes were wet. While we were doing pushups, I noticed a dragon fly trying to climb in my nose and thought to myself, yeah climb in there and die of heat exposure, but it flew off to a cooler clime.

When we completed the exercises we were divided into groups defined by our hoped-for team position. I had never been anything but a lineman. All through pee wee football and junior high the coaches took one look at my big ass and tackle here I came. This choice of positions would always be quickly confirmed when we were timed in 40-yard sprints. There was no danger of my ever touching the football unless I blocked a punt or covered a fumble. That suited me fine. I just liked to hit.

Coach Willy Slade was the line coach and he gathered us around to deliver his philosophic thoughts on the intricacies of line play. They were simple. Knock the shit out of the guy across from you, sort through the rest of them for the dude with the football and smash his ass. Slade had played tackle at Tennessee and he was a strict disciple of Coach Neyland. Three yards and a cloud of bloody dust.

Coach Slade went on to add, "We ain't gonna have any contact this morning; that'll come this afternoon. We're gonna knock off for a couple of hours at noon and get started again at 2:00. All that's left this morning is a light workout on the blocking sled. Any questions?"

One of the new guys, Larry Ward, raised his hand and Coach Slade told him to go on with his question.

"Coach, it's awful hot out here, any chance that we can get some water?"

Coach Willy Slade was a very big man, maybe 6'6" and close to 275 lbs. He was wearing athletic shorts and football shoes without a shirt, just a whistle around his neck. Slade had jet black curly hair, not just on his head, but all over. The summer sun had toasted him to a betel nut brown. I bet he had hair on the palm of his hands. His face was creased by a jutting Neanderthal brow with one uninterrupted huge eyebrow. In spite of his bulk he started to swell up even bigger. His eyes bulged, his face turned purple and a vein the size of garden hose began to throb in his neck.

"Did you just ask me for water?" he managed to sputter.

"Yes coach. But it's no big thing; in fact, I really don't want any water." The rookie was looking for an escape route, but it was clear that his question did not sit well with Coach Slade.

Coach Slade walked over to the offender and jerked him to his feet by grabbing his pads in one of his bear paws.

"You need some water? Well, by God we'll get you some." He roared.

"The rest of you form a single file right here in front of this thirsty lad."

Benny and I were about mid way in the line, which seemed to be the safest place to hide. Coach Slade looked at us and said,

"Here we have an opportunity to extend a helping hand to a team mate in distress, I want each of you to walk up to this thirsty lad and spit in his mouth."

As we did this, Slade looked the group up and down and said,

"I hope y'all got the message here: THERE AIN'T GONNA BE ANY GODDAMN WATER!"

Once we had saved Larry from dehydration, we were directed to the two-man blocking sled. This device had been developed in the The Marquis de Sade's lab and further perfected by Dr. Joseph Mengele. I am certain that the Geneva Convention had not been consulted. It consisted of an aluminum pan about six feet in diameter, with two padded, spring-loaded blocking posts welded to the bottom and extending about five feet above the ground. There was enough room for a coach to stand on the device and hang onto the blocking post.

The concept was simple; two linemen would assume a four-point stance, and upon the whistle signal from the on-board coach, smash into the blocking post with a shoulder and drive with their legs, thus propelling the device downfield. Then came the bad news. We were going to take the sled for a complete circuit of the field, the same route we had earlier run. The good news was that we only had to do this once.

Slade's whistle sounded and off we went. By the time we had finished driving the sled and returned to the end of the line it was time to go again. We made the one lap circuit and each of us staggered and swayed with exhaustion; we were close to heat stroke.

Slade's whistle sounded. It was noon and the morning session had come an end. All that was left were a few fifty-yard wind sprints.

"He's got to be kidding" I said.

"I don't think so, and I damn sure don't plan to ask." Benny replied.

We each ran four fifty-yard sprints. "Ran" might be a stretch; actually we stumbled, staggered and in some cases crawled through the drill. I didn't know I could be so hot and tired. My head was spinning and my vision was beginning to blur. I barely heard Coach Wiley's whistle.

The whole team gathered around him and he told us to take a knee. A couple of guys were down flat. They could have been dead.

"Listen up. We are going to knock off and start our afternoon session at two o'clock sharp. This will give y'all a chance to grab some lunch and rehydrate. For you new guys, I would suggest you choose your lunch carefully; you'll probably see it coming back up this afternoon. This morning was just a light workout; this afternoon we get serious. See y'all at two."

I looked at Benny and said,

"So, that was a light workout, huh?"

"Just a bit of conditioning," Benny agreed, "and as soon as I can walk or crawl, I'm going to head for the locker room."

We gained our feet and began walking slowly across the parking lot to the gym. We noticed that the managers were standing along the sidewalk instructing everyone to strip out of their uniforms and lay them out in the sun to dry before the next session started. We stripped down to our jocks and went into the locker room. I lost the jock and was heading to the showers when I heard my name being called. I looked up to see Jesse Carr motioning me over to his locker.

Now what? I wondered.

I walked over to Jesse's locker awaiting his instructions. In addition to being an NCO in the Guard, he dated the big sister of a girl I had a serious crush on. We had crossed paths a couple of times, not that he had paid much attention to me.

"Well, rookie, this is your lucky day." He said with a big grin. "You've been given the opportunity of a lifetime, a chance to serve and learn at the feet of the master. This is a good-news, bad-news deal. The bad news is you have to keep my stuff in perfect shape, my shoes clean, cleaned and polished, my gear clean and in good working order and my locker fully supplied. The good news is that in return, I will teach you the tricks of the trade and make your life a lot more pleasant and a helluva lot more interesting. Any questions?"

"No, it seems clear enough" I said, fearing that any question would result in something akin to Coach Slade's tirade.

"Good, clean up this mess before you go eat, and meet me back here before we take the field this afternoon. See ya later." I had been dismissed.

As I started to pick up Jesse's wet towels and other crap, Benny called to me from the shower room door.

"Come quick, you gotta see this. You just ain't gonna believe it."

About twenty guys were milling around the entrance to the shower room attempting to look as nonchalant as possible, but all were staring intently at the huge, hairy naked body of Willy Slade enjoying a hot shower all by himself. Seeing a Yeti *au naturale* was in and of itself interesting; seeing one with a wanger the size of a fungo bat was something else altogether. Willy Slade was hung like a Clydesdale; he would probably pass out from loss of blood if he ever got that monster fully pumped up. Willy gave a whole new definition to "penis envy".

Benny interrupted my anatomical musings, and said, "Let's go over to the Kreme Freeze and grab some lunch, it's already 12:40 and we gotta be back in just over an hour."

We hit the shower, threw on our shorts and tee shirts and walked across the schoolyard to the local hang out. The Kreme Freeze catered to the school crowd almost exclusively. The food was pretty good if you liked hamburgers and fried onion rings. They had good shakes, malts and soft serve ice cream. I probably ate half of my meals at the Kreme Freeze.

Benny ordered a cheeseburger, fries and a chocolate shake. The boy was fearless.

"I suppose you missed the part about throwing all that up this afternoon." I said, as I ordered a double dip soft serve and a cup of crushed ice.

"No, I heard it, I just don't care. I'll enjoy it going down and try to ignore it if I see it later on. I'm hungry enough to eat the ass end out of Willy Slade."

"That should be enough to make you barf on the spot. That ain't hungry, that's plain sick."

"It's a figure of speech, asshead."

"Now that's comforting to know. I'll be haunted all afternoon by the image of your head gnawing on Willy's ass."

Benny's burger came and we ate in silence, slumped in the vinyl booth listening to Kitty Kallen's Little Things Mean a Lot.

It was 1:30 before we knew it and time to go get suited up. We gathered our gear from the sidewalk and sure enough it was totally dry. It didn't smell so great, but it was dry. After I had everything on, I carried my helmet and walked over to Jesse's locker. Jesse was sitting on the bench tying his shoes and looking fresh and rested. Nothing seemed to bother him much. He looked up and handed me half of a lemon.

"Stick this in the webbing of your helmet. Suck on it when you start getting cotton mouth. It'll help. Just don't get caught with it, they'll make you eat it. When practice is over and you get everything done, meet me at my car in the parking lot. "

I said, "Thanks for the lemon, I'll see you after we get in," and went back to our locker. I took my pocket knife and split the lemon in quarters, giving one to Benny with the same instructions. We headed to the practice field. Waves of heat radiated from the asphalt parking lot causing mini mirages and false horizons. The humidity remained in the nineties, but any semblance of moisture was over powered by the sun's relentless hammering.

Coach Wiley blew his whistle and the whole shebang began a spirited circuit of the practice field, the coaches and the managers following closely behind. I noticed that there were a few less runners than we started with this morning. Clearly a sense of survival had overcome dreams of athletic glory for about a half dozen campers. They would never be mentioned.

This was the hottest part of the day, and the morning's smell of fresh cut grass had given way to the singed, heat-seared aroma of plants being cooked in their own juice. There were no birds singing, no insects humming and very little sound of human activity. All God's creatures were hiding in the shade until the heat index got below 101 °F. Well, not all of God's creatures, there were some fifty-odd idiots running around like mad dogs.

The run was going better from what Benny and I could see from the middle of the pack. About twenty guys were ahead of us and all seemed to be okay. What was going on behind us we couldn't say. When we made the turn to start the second lap, we could see the coaches and managers driving the stragglers forward with the same methods the Japs had employed on the Bataan death march. Cruel, but it seemed to be working. No one had stopped, but several were throwing up and looking like they were in shock.

By the fourth lap we had moved a little closer to the front, and I realized that Jesse Carr was leading the run looking like he had just stepped out of the air conditioning. The son-of-a-bitch didn't sweat. Jesse played center on offense, linebacker on defense and had lettered in the ninth and tenth grade. Leadership just came naturally to Jesse and he was clearly going to be a team leader in this, his junior year.

We completed the run with everyone crossing the finish line, some with a lot of help, but finishing with the rest of us. We moved rapidly through the jumping jacks and pushups, and soon we lineman were back under the scowl of Coach Slade. He blew his whistle and rallied us up. The fun was about to begin.

Our first drill was known affectionately known as" two-on-one", one guy would get down in a four-point stance facing two others. When the whistle sounded the two would double team the one and try to crush him into the dusty field. The one's job was to defeat the double team and hold his ground. There was no way that everyone succeeded and the losers were met with harsh judgment by Coach Slade. You went back to the line, rinsed and repeated.

This wasn't my first rodeo. We had been doing this drill on every football team I had ever played on and I knew the ropes. I was 5ft 9in and had weighed 188 lbs when we took our physicals that morning. The two oafs across from me were both well over six feet tall and one of them was a real tub of lard at about 240 lbs. They had that look of blood lust usually associated with bull fighting. I could see overconfidence oozing out of every pore. They were going to crush my ass.

We assumed the four-point stance and the whistle blew. They clearly expected me to rise up and try to fend them off. Instead I submarined under their charge and hit the lard bucket with a sharp forearm to the gut, butting the other one in the face with my old leather helmet. I kept my feet under me and my legs driving until Coach Slade blew his whistle. Blubber butt was bent over with his hands on his knees wheezing and the other dude was looking like he had never had a nose bleed before. I jogged to the back of the line without looking at Coach Slade. When I turned around he was looking at me with a quizzical stare. He shook his head and smiled.

I noticed that the other guys treated me with a little reserve as we continued the drill. No one seemed intent on crushing me. It doesn't take much to make a statement and mark your territory. I knew I had made the team that afternoon. From the two-on-one drill we went through some technique drills for defensive and offensive linemen working on individual skills until about 4:00. I had several opportunities to sneak a suck on my lemon quarter and darned if it didn't help. It was still hot as hell, but the worst part of the day was done.

Coach Wiley rallied us up and said that the next part of the afternoon would be spent working on running plays with blocking dummies. The defensive players would each hold a one-man dummy and the offense would fire out and carry through their blocking assignments. There would be no actual contact. As we started to jog off to join the B team drills, Coach Slade said,

"Larch, you stay over here with the A bunch for a while."

It was my intention to never go back down the ladder. After all we had an 8-2 record on our junior high team and these turkeys had gone 0-10. I could play with this bunch.

Cumberland, like most high school and college teams still ran the single wing, and there was not much mystery involved on either side of the ball. On offense it was designed to put a pulling guard, a fullback and a blocking back at the point of attack and steamroll the outmanned defensive player. The job of the defensive linemen was just as simple, penetrate the neutral zone and knock down some of that wedge of blockers. The defensive ends were on a suicide mission on every play, don't let anybody outside, and use your body to knock down the wall of blockers. The linebackers and the corner backs should make most of the tackles.

My afternoon didn't last all that long. About midway through the live scrimmage I was playing head up between the lard ass and Jesse Carr, the starting center. I noticed that the lard ass across from me would change his stance slightly if he were trying to block me left or right. He was trying to gain that little edge, and I had been wearing his ass out all afternoon. On what proved to be the last play of the day for me, I could see that he was not cheating to either side. This meant that the play was probably going right at me. It could be a direct snap to the fullback or a spinner play with the tail back handing the ball off to the fullback. Option three was that blubber butt would allow me to penetrate the neutral zone unopposed where I would be met by a pulling guard and the fullback in a trap play. The blocking back would take on the inside linebacker and the tailback would run to glory.

I'd been having a pretty good scrimmage, and I figured the coaching staff felt that it was time to bring me down a notch or two. This was going to be a trap play, and I had the advantage of knowing it was coming. Jesse snapped the ball. Blubber butt faked a little block on me, before lumbering off to try and block one of our linebackers. Instead of sailing through the gap left for me, I turned and met the pulling guard head on before he could get up a good head of steam. As soon as I made contact with the guard I spun to my right to find the charging fullback. I found him with my head on his thigh pad at full speed. My lights went out.

There was a sharp acrid and overpowering burning in my nose. I opened my eyes to small pin pricks of light that began to open up like the lens of a camera. I could see blue sky and what appeared to be a small cylinder with tape on it under my nose. I tried to sit up, but for some reason I could not find my hands and feet. Coach Slade's big hairy face filled my view. I suppose he was talking to me, but all I could hear was a loud ringing in my ears. I noticed a sharp coppery taste in my mouth and felt a warm liquid running down my chin. I finally heard what Coach Slade was asking me,

"How many fingers am I holding up?" He asked.

I immediately answered "Thursday" with a big grin. Then the lights went out again.

I finally came around in the locker room enough to see that everyone was off the field and milling about showering and getting dressed. I was lying on a training table with my head wrapped in a towel full of ice and two stitches in my lower lip. I could see Tommy Carter standing by the table smiling at me. Tommy was a rookie manager and one of my best friends.

"Larch, you had us pretty concerned for a while there. They stitched up your lip and you never seemed to notice it. You took a pretty good lick on your big ole hard head. By the way, I threw your lemon away before anyone saw it. It was smashed flat."

"Thanks, I gotta get up and get outta here. I need to clean up Jesse's locker, get a shower and meet him in the parking lot."

I sat up on the side of the table and the room started to spin crazily. I shook my head and the room settled back to its normal position. I pulled the towel off and eased to my feet. I tried a couple of steps and shakily made my way to my locker. Benny and Jesse Carr were standing by the locker deep in conversation. When I walked up, Jesse said,

"Don't worry about my stuff tonight, you can come in early tomorrow and take care of it. Grab a shower. I want you guys to come with me for about 30 minutes and then I'll take y'all home. You can put your bikes in the back of my pickup."

"Just give me a minute," I replied, and we'll be right along. Meet you in the parking lot."

"What's that all about?" I asked Benny.

"Beats the hell outta me. He wanted to be sure we would meet him before we went home. Probably got some more stuff he wants you to do. By the way, you are the star of the day, and you pissed off a lot of people."

"Screw em if they can't take a joke. Football 's a contact sport, ya know."

"Well George Binds made plenty of contact with your head, that's for sure."

"Did we stop the play?"

"Oh, yeah, Herbert threw them for a two yard loss. Was it worth getting your bell rung?"

" You bet it was worth it. Like I said, 'it's a contact sport'. That cuts both ways"

"How do you feel? Sure you don't have a concussion? How many fingers am I holding up?" he said, extending his middle finger in my face.

"April," I replied with a grin.

I showered and the cold water seemed to revive me even more. My lip hurt a little, but I suspect the Novocain was still working. Amazingly, I had no headache. After I pulled on my shorts, shirt and tennis shoes, Benny and I met Jesse at his truck. We loaded our bikes in the back and jumped in the cab.

"Where are we going?" I asked as we pulled out of the school parking lot and headed toward Cumberland's two-street downtown area.

"You'll see." Jesse said, driving across the tracks to the seamy side of town. I was betting on Katz's pool hall, but we passed it heading east. We finally pulled into the gravel parking lot of Andy's Tap Room.

There was very little chance that we would run into our Dads in Andy's. Benny's old man was probably at the Country Club decompressing in the 19th hole and mine was just as surely playing gin at the VFW Club with all of his WWII buddies. Both would not be going home until well after seven. We entered Andy's close on Jesse's tail.

Andy's was cool, dark and smelled faintly of French fries and stale beer, not at all unpleasant, kind of exotic to our untrained senses. There were neon lights everywhere. Signs hawking Budweiser, Schlitz, Miller's , Jax and a couple that were new to me. The pinball machines were all in use, as was the shuffle board table. It was high cocktail hour, and in Cumberland that meant plenty of beer. Jesse took a stool at the bar and motioned for us to join him.

We settled in and he turned to Andy, "Give us three draughts and a couple of packages of pretzels, if you will, kind sir."

Andy looked at Benny and me, turned to Jesse and said, "Carr, how old are these two?"

"Old enough, Andy, they are both in the 155th. If they are old enough to fight, they are surely old enough to have a beer."

"In the Guard are they? Well that's good enough for me," and he pulled three 16oz draughts in frosted mugs.

"Here's to your first day of football. You both really did well."

The first sip of that frosty beer was a life changing event. The cold foam and golden brew slide down my gullet like honey to a bee. I may live to be a hundred, but that first cold beer remains one of the great joys of my life. Jesse entertained us with stories about football and working at the East Implement Company. He had been on his own since his Dad had been killed in a gun fight under some very strange circumstances. He never mentioned his father, but he kept us in stitches while we finished our beers. I was ready to get another round, but Jesse said not tonight. Tonight was a special occasion and one would be enough.

By the time Jesse dropped us off at the edge of City Park about a block from Benny's house, I would l have been willing to stand in the middle of Highway 61 and gone one-on-one with the truck traffic. I had my first role model and he would turn out to be a doozy. Benny and I rode to his house and said good night. I told him that I would meet him in the morning, but thirty minutes earlier. I still had to clean up Jesse's locker.

I rode the three blocks to my house and parked my bike in the carport. I came in the back door just as my mother was putting supper on the table. Dad looked up from reading the Memphis Press Scimitar and said,

"What did you do today?"

"Not much," I answered," I got a paper you need to sign for me."

"Last paper I signed you ended up in the Guard; what now?"

"Nothin' much, just permission to play football."

"I wish you wouldn't do that," my mother said," What's wrong with trying out for the band? You could get hurt playing football."

"Leave the boy alone, Kathleen. Let him play ball. God knows, he can't carry a tune."

Hello Colonel Lee

The invitations started to show up in the mail in early October. The *Delta Subdebutante Club* announced its 1953 Christmas Cotillion Season. There would be Christmas dances in six different Delta towns sharing several things in common. All of the young ladies in the club would attend all of the dances, as would the young men on the invitation list. All of the dances would be followed by a German Breakfast at the home of a local subdeb, all would be formal and would feature the music of the Red Tops.

It would have been safe to assume that the prospect of sixty or so teenage girls, dressed to the nines and herded up in one place, would be incentive enough to attract a hundred or so testosterone-crazed teenage boys, and it certainly was. The presence of the Red Tops made sure that attendance would be near one hundred percent.

The Red Tops were a six-man dance orchestra. They played music ranging from the big band standards to current popular music just touching the edge of rhythm and blues. They passed the parental censors by taking it easy on the rock and roll. The Red Tops' featured vocalist was tenor Rufus McKay. He could have been a huge recording star if he had accepted the many offers to come to New York or Nashville and cut a record. Rufus had no intention of ever setting foot on an airplane, and it was deemed too far to drive. The Red Tops stayed at home in Vicksburg and were booked almost every night.

Benny and I were sitting on his bed looking at the stack of invitations we had received over the past month. There were dances planned starting in Rosedale on November 13th and every Saturday night until the grand finale in Lexington on December 18th.

"Why don't we go to them all, which would give us six shots to get lucky?" he said.

"Yeah, a total of 180 at bats, even when you factor in the 5-3 odds, still a statistically target-rich environment."

"Another plus is the parent chaperone system they use; having marriage obsessed mothers guarding the hormone-crazed hen house is like asking John Dillinger to join the bank's board. The whole point of these soirees is aimed at matrimony somewhere down the trail."

I grinned and said, "Marriage isn't real high on my planning agenda, but I am more than willing to host auditions in the back seat of your Dad's new car."

"I guess we'll have to buy a tux since all of these are formal. I hate to spend my rat hole on clothes."

"Look at it this way, if you were about to go duck hunting for the first time you would need a hell'va lot more expensive gear. A tux probably cost less than a good pair of waders. It's just six more hunting trips and you can't screw a duck, at least most people would think it unsportsmanlike."

"When you put it like that, it makes a lot more sense. You can't spend too much on waders; one morning with ice cold water in your shorts will convince you of that. I would hate to miss bagging a debutante because I didn't have the proper gear."

"That's the spirit! Let's go to Kaplan's and see what we're up against on this tux business."

The commercial area of downtown Cumberland was built on two sides of a square; the other two sides were bounded by my grandfather's old ice plant, now abandoned, and the main line of the Illinois Central Railroad. There was a municipal park in the center and Ike Kaplan's small department store was on the east side of the park.

Benny and I walked into Kaplan's and were immediately greeted by a stout little man with a measuring tape hung around his neck like a doctor with a stethoscope. Ike Kaplan knew his market. He stocked everything from baby stuff all the way to an outfit suitable for burial. The funeral suit was comprised of a white shirt, a tie and a black suit coat and a pair of underwear. Ike couldn't see the point of including pants, belts, shoes or socks. The coffin would not be fully opened and who'd ever know?

He was also the only official purveyor of Boy Scout gear in this part of the Delta, and he carried a full selection of high quality hunting and fishing gear. If Ike didn't have it, he could get it for you.

"Ah, two of my favorite young customers," Ike beamed, "what will it be today, Boy Scout Uniforms or hunting clothes?"

"Actually, we're interested in looking at tuxedos," I said.

"Oh, of course, it's time for the debutante dances. I'm sure I can fix you up with just what you need."

Ike had a teenage daughter named Ruth. Benny and I had gone to school with Ruth since the first grade and thought she was a really neat gal. Ruth was probably the smartest kid in our class, she was absolutely beautiful and maybe the kindest person we knew. Ruth had not been invited to join the Cotillion club; Jewish girls were not eligible. Ruth would be going to Memphis and Atlanta to attend the big holiday dances held by the Jewish youth organizations.

Ike led us to the back of the store and said, "Benny, step up on that little platform and let me get your measurements."

He measured here and there, humming to himself and jotting down stuff in a small notebook. Finally he finished with Benny and motioned me to step up. When he completed my measurements he said,

"Well, I believe we're in luck today. Benny you'll need a 34 long and Tommy you need a 42 long. I think I have both in stock, let me check."

He came back carrying two black suits encased in vinyl travel bags with "Kaplan's of Cumberland" printed on them. He hung the bags on hooks and said,

"There are a couple of alternatives you need to consider and I want to give you my opinion. I carry After Six which is one of the top brands of ready to wear formal clothing. It is first quality material and skilled workmanship. An After Six tux should last a lifetime, assuming reasonable use, proper care, and prudent eating habits. An After Six would cost you $150.00 plus tax. Alterations are free. In addition to the tux, you'll need the accessories such as a formal shirt, a cummerbund, silk socks, black lace-up shoes, a tie, studs and cufflinks. If you choose accessories of the same quality as After Six, your total package would come in close to $250.00."

We must have looked like a duck being hit with a wooden spoon. We were in severe sticker shock.

"However, there is another route you can go. You are both rapidly growing young men and you will probably outgrow whatever you buy today within a year or two. I think you should consider the other option. I also stock a line of formal wear made in Hong Kong. The material is not as fine as After Six and the workmanship is at best acceptable. I can tailor these suits to look just as good as an After Six; they just won't last as long. They come with a complete set of accessories and cost only $129.00. My recommendation is to buy the Hong Kong ensemble."

$129.00 was more than either of us could afford, but compared to $250.00, it seemed to be a God-send.

"Mr. Kaplan, I agree that we ought to get the less expensive tux, but we have an additional problem. Neither one of us has $129.00. We can probably come up with $75.00 each."

"Tell you what I'll do," Ike said. "I'll sell you the outfits and put them on a one year credit plan. You give me $75.00 down and I'll spread the remaining $54.00, plus a small interest charge, over twelve monthly payments of $5.00 each."

"The only money that Benny and I get is an allowance from our parents and any summer job we can find. We do get our National Guard check every three months and I guess we could use it to pay you."

"How much is your Guard check?"

"It's usually about $30.00, give or take, depending on how many drills are in the quarter."

"Okay, here's what we can do. I'll make the payments quarterly and you can make them with your Guard checks. I'll take $18.00 per quarter and you boys can keep the difference. You will be all paid up by this time next year."

Benny nodded his agreement to the plan and I said, "Mr. Kaplan, you got a deal. Will the tuxes be ready by a week from Friday?"

"Let me pin them up this afternoon and I'll see that they're ready to go in time. It won't take another ten minutes to pin them and you can be on your way."

Not a bad afternoon's work, I thought, fancy new duds and our first charge accounts. Look out girls, we're on our way.

Ike delivered the tuxedos just as promised and added a white summer tux jacket as lagniappe. The big day was here, and about 4:00pm on Saturday afternoon I decided to bathe and get dressed for the dance. I was standing in my bedroom in my skivvies, staring at the whole formal outfit removed from its packaging and laid out on my bed. I had no idea where to start.

Normally, I would put my socks on next and that seemed to be a good plan. I unfolded the flimsy faux silk socks and slipped them on my feet. They felt like no socks at all. I was wondering if I should slip on a pair of white athletic socks and pull the little black numbers on over them; at least I wouldn't get blisters from dancing.

I was pondering this plan when the door to my room opened and Dad walked in. He closed the door and sat on the edge of my bed and said,

"I'll bet you could use some help figuring that monkey suit out."

"You bet I could, I don't even know what all this stuff is for. I think Ike gave me a faulty shirt, it doesn't have enough buttons down the front and the sleeves are way too long, not to mention having no cuff buttons."

"The shirt should be your next move. Slip it on just like a regular shirt."

I pulled the shirt on and stood there with it buttoned near my navel and the cuffs hanging 4" past my hands. This was clearly not going to work.

"Okay," Dad said, "this is a little tricky. Let's deal with the French cuffs first. Fold back the cuffs to align the button holes on the bottom part with the button holes on the top. Open that little black box and there should be two cuff links and five studs in it. The cuff links are bigger than the studs."

"I got 'em. What now?"

"You'll see the little toggle device on the stems, put it in the vertical position. This should form a straight shaft. Stick the shaft through all four layers of cuff material and move the toggle to lock behind the last layer."

I followed his instructions and got the cuff links locked into place and said,

"Why ever would you want to button your shirt cuff with something mechanical? Besides, it looks dumb with that toggle thingamajig showing."

"Tommy, you've got them in backwards. Turn them around where the shiny black circle faces out."

We worked our way through the studs, which I had to admit looked pretty cool in place of buttons. I was standing there in my skivvies with my open-collared shirt on admiring myself in the mirror.

"What's next?" I asked.

"Let's get the pants on."

I pulled the black pants over my silk socks and noticed that there was a black shinny ribbon running the length of the pair of pants. That's pretty cool, I thought. I started to button the pants and Dad said,

"Don't button up until you get the suspenders on."

That was the first time I had noticed the set of white suspenders that had been packed with the black tie. The only suspenders I had ever worn were the snap on kind with my bird hunting pants. These did not have snaps, but two pieces of leather with button holes at the end of all four parts. I was completely baffled.

"It would be best to put the suspenders on before you pull the pants on. Lay them on the bed and hook the suspenders to the two buttons on each side front and back." Of course I did them upside down the first time, but I finally caught on. I pulled the pants up and snapped the suspenders into place. The rest of the deal was fairly intuitive and soon I was fully dressed. I was surprised at how comfortable the whole rig was. I had nothing binding or tugging on me with complete freedom of movement. I have loved wearing a tux ever since.

My mother insisted that I pose for a couple of snapshots to send to my grandparents, and I tried to look like I dressed like this every day. Soon the photos were done and we were working our way through the long version of the "Be Careful" speech. My Dad just rolled his eyes and kept his mouth shut; this wasn't his first goat roping.

She finished off the mother hen routine and said,

"You're not driving, are you?"

"No ma'am, Benny and I are riding over with Jimmy Hogan. His Dad just got a new Pontiac and he's letting him use it tonight.

"Jimmy Hogan is too young to be driving an automobile. I think your father should drive you."

That brought my Dad back into the conversation. He planned to play gin rummy tonight.

"Good God, Kathleen, Hogan is fifteen and has his driver's license. It's only nineteen miles of perfectly straight paved highway. What the hell could happen in nineteen miles?"

"The State of Mississippi might be stupid enough to allow a fifteen-year-old to drive, but that doesn't mean we should allow our fifteen-year-old to ride with him."

I had witnessed enough of these parental discussions to know that after my Mother had her say, she would relent, and give in to the plan. Of course she never forgot the conversation and was real big on "I told you so".

The debate was drawing to a close when a horn sounded in front of the house. Hogan was here to pick me up. I kissed my mother and winked at my father who handed me a ten dollar bill as I headed for the front door. The evening had begun to get downright chilly and the forecast called for a hard freeze overnight. I was the last guy to be picked up and this put me in the middle position in the back of the car.

"Hey, everybody" I said, "What's the plan?"

"We got a little errand to run before we head out to Rosedale," Hogan said.

"Oh yeah, what's that?"

"We got to fuel up for the evening."

That made sense; we didn't want to run out of gas. We headed in the direction of Luper Cole's Gulf Station on Highway 61 and drove right by it.

"Where in the hell do you buy gas?" I asked.

"Who said anything about gas? The old man gave it to me full. We're heading to Johnny Dolan's for our fuel."

Johnny Dolan was the local bootlegger. Mississippi was officially a dry state, but it allowed and taxed a network of bootleggers, some of which were stocked better than Martin's Wine Cellar in New Orleans. Dolan was a bit more modest. He operated out of an old wooden store in a cotton field on the edge of town. There were two modes of service at Dolan's. You could pull up in the gravel parking lot and toot your horn. Man, Dolan's black major domo, would come out and take your order, then deliver it to your car. You were expected to give Man a generous tip.

We chose the self-service option. We pulled the car to a window on the side of the shack and Man slid it open.

"What's your pleasure, boys?" He grinned.

It was perfectly obvious that we were rookies concerning bootleggers; we had no idea about what to ask for. Man looked at us and said, "Y'all must be heading to the dance in Rosedale. We been doing a bunch of business with boys in tuxes tonight. Most are buying Colonel Lee by the half-pint. If you just sip along on it, you can keep a buzz all evening."

Hogan looked around the car and no one had a better idea, so he said, "Man, make it six half-pints of Colonel Lee, how much are they?"

"They be eighty-five cents apiece. That'll be $5.10 total," Man did the math in his head without hesitation. One might surmise this was not his first night on the job.

We all came up with a dollar each and Hogan told Man to keep the change and said,

"We still got a while before we need to head to Rosedale, let's go to the El Rancho and get some ice and cokes."

When we drove into the gravel parking lot of the El Rancho we saw several cars loaded with our friends. We were soon sitting at one of the large tables in the back and had placed our orders for ice and cokes. My Dad had always told me that there were two secrets to successful drinking. Learn to nurse a drink along, sip, don't guzzle, and drink enough to get on the edge of the wave, but don't drink enough to crash. I had no idea exactly what he was talking about, but I knew for sure that when it came to drinking whiskey he was a world-class authority.

I decided to put a couple of cubes of ice in a water glass and try the sipping plan. I broke the seal on the half pint of Colonel Lee and experienced a life changing moment. The rich, aroma wafting from the little bottle hit my olfactory senses like the Mormon Tabernacle Choir singing the Hallelujah Chorus. A half century later, I am truly convinced that this was the exact moment that I became an alcoholic. The smell of Colonel Lee hit every Irish gene in my DNA and launched a thirty year love affair with booze. All of this, and I hadn't even tasted it yet.

I was no longer conscious of my fellow drinkers; it was just me and Colonel Lee. I poured about three fingers into the glass of ice and swirled it around before taking the first sip. If the aroma had been the Hallelujah Chorus, then the taste registered somewhere between the Ode to Joy and the climax of the 1812 Overture. I immediately understood what my Dad was talking about, this was to be sipped and savored, not polluted with Coca-Cola or some other garbage.

I was in a world apart. After the third sip I felt warmth behind my knees that began to spread up my legs and into my stomach. Soon my entire psyche was bathed in a sense of well-being that reminded me of the first few moments following orgasm when all of the endorphins flood your system. Now I understood the concept of staying on the edge of the wave. In less than five minutes I had become a seasoned drinker. I thought I would drink whiskey for the rest of my life, but Bill Wilson screwed up that plan.

I was snatched back to reality by Jimmy Hogan pushing his chair over and slamming his fist on the table top.

"By God! A half pint is not nearly enough to last the evening, I'm going back and get a fifth. Anybody want to go with me?"

I had taken exactly three sips at this point and figured I wouldn't need any more. Besides, Benny was drinking beer, which he loved, and hadn't bothered to open his half pint. I could probably have it if I needed it.

"You guys go on, but be sure to come back and pick us up. Benny and I will hold down the fort here."

The four of them left, laughing and pushing on each other as they bounded into Hogan's car and disappeared in the direction of Dolan's. Benny took a deep drink of beer and said,

"I suspect one of us will end up driving to Rosedale; those guys polished off a half pint in about five minutes and are going for more. I'm no expert, but my guess is that they will soon crash and burn. I still want to go to the dance."

Within five minutes the group had returned with a fifth of Early Times and fixed another round of drinks. They were having a great time laughing and horse-playing, and the level in the Early Times bottle dropped precipitously. I was still on my first drink and Benny had ordered a second beer. For the first time I experienced the dynamic of a bunch of drunks. The whiskey had a different effect on each of them.

Joe Mosley became silent and downright sullen. His eyes had an eerie gleam and darted all about the room as if looking for a target. Joe was a hot-headed guy when he was sober, and drinking seemed to accentuate his hostility.

Donald Meagher was laughing out loud; the more he drank, the funnier things got. The whisky sent him into gales of laughter, and soon he was just giggling to himself. Donald was a happy drunk.

Les Jones had settled into a comfortable position with his head on the table and had all the appearances of a man finished for the evening.

Hogan was still going strong. He mixed still another drink and announced,

"You guys save my place, I gotta piss like Man o' War."

He stood up, took two steps and crashed to the floor in a crumpled heap. I looked at Benny and said,

"This looks like a good time to be on our way to Rosedale. Help me head 'em up and move 'em out."

Joe, Benny and I carried Hogan and Jones and propped them up in the backseat. We took the car keys out of Hogan's pocket and put the half-empty fifth in the glove compartment. Donald was still giggling to himself, and we convinced him to sit in back and take care of the stiffs. Benny drove, I took shotgun and Joe sat sullenly in the middle. We hit Highway 8 and took off for the dance.

The gala was being held at the Rosedale Country Club, and the first thing on the agenda was listed as a "Mixer" scheduled to start at 8:00 and lasting till 9:00 when the Red Tops would crank it up. We were going to be a little late for the mixer, but I felt that this group had done quite enough mixing already. At about 8:35 we pulled into the Country Club parking lot.

All three of the campers in the back seat were passed out. We decided to let them sleep it off. Benny took the car keys and we headed to what remained of the mixer. In the foyer of the club we were confronted by a large table manned by several of the mother/chaperones and one of the ladies pinned a name tag to the left lapel of our tux jackets. We wandered into the main ball room where sixty young ladies, their mothers and fathers and one hundred or so young swains were awkwardly shuffling around.

If you have ever been quail hunting and let the bird dogs out of their crate to run loose among the waiting birds, you would have some idea of Benny's reaction to this plethora of Delta maidens. He began to circle the crowd looking for a target. He raised his head as if to test the air for the telltale scent of estrogen. I fully expected him to start marking his area by peeing in the corners of the room. It was a thing of beauty to watch a hunter working the flock.

Benny was born a ladies' man. He had that sleepy eyed look and lopsided grin that made women want to leave their husbands and children and devote their lives to trying to screw Benny to death.

He was also one of those natural-born dancers. He had never had a dance lesson in his life; it just came to him like pointing a covey was instinctive to a bird dog. On the dance floor Benny was grace and confidence; he could take the plainest and most awkward girl in the room and transform her into Ginger Rogers. This lad was in his element.

I, on the other hand, danced like a bear with a poker up his ass. I'm tone deaf and have no sense of rhythm. The choir director at Grace Episcopal Church had asked me not to sing the hymns and chants. She said that I was so off key, that mine was the only voice she could hear and it was driving her mad. My mother had tried to teach me some basic dance steps, but she had about the same results as my Dad did when he tried to teach me golf. After a whole summer of instruction he finally said,

"Tommy, I believe the only way you'll ever be able to play golf is for us to break your arms and have them reset. Even then I doubt you'd be worth a damn. Why don't you stick to trying to learn how to play defensive tackle? There may be hope for you there."

I danced just like I played golf, but I did not anticipate that this would be a problem since I didn't intend to dance. Coupled with the fact that I was such a lousy dancer, I fully understood that I did my best work in a one-on-one situation, and I intended to take maximum advantage of the breaks to check out the field.

About nine o'clock the Red Tops started moving their instruments onto the bandstand. They were dressed in their signature Red tux jackets and it was clear that this was something they loved to do. Soon the band started the evening with their old standard, The Sheik of Araby, (With no pants on). And the evening was underway.

I stood on the edge of the dance floor watching the rhythmic flow of dancing bodies throb and bob to the music. I kept an eye out for Benny while letting the brassy sounds roll over me like waves on the beach. I was just grooving along when I noticed a couple dancing just beyond my reach. I came eye to eye with the loveliest creature I had ever seen.

She was a dark-haired girl with a slender body and penetrating brown eyes. If every young man has a dozen or so traits that comprise the perfect girl, this little beauty hit all of mine. I was looking at the love of my life, and I knew it instantly. I must have looked like I'd been hit in the head by a Bob Feller fast-ball. My eye caught hers and something passed between us that can't be explained. She moved away into the dancing crowd and left me paralyzed in her wake.

I moved across the room as the Red Tops began to play Moon Glow and the dancers settled into a slow dance holding each other close. I found a position that allowed me to watch her as she nestled in the arms of her partner. I wanted to kill him. He was a rosy cheeked young man about 5'9" and 140 pounds. He looked like he might play trumpet in the band and was probably class president. I hated his guts.

I finally regained my composure and decided to mount an offensive aimed at winning the attention, if not the heart, of the girl of my dreams. First I needed to know her name and where she was from. For this intelligence I could rely on my childhood buddy and confidant Mary Agnes Barnes. Mary Agnes was a grade ahead of me and knew everything worth knowing and a whole bunch of useless stuff as well.

I tracked Mary Agnes down at the punch bowl and her eyes lit up when she saw me coming her way.

"Tommy," she cooed, "just the guy I wanted to see. I bet you've got something to help this awful punch."

"I do indeed," I said, patting the half pint in my jacket pocket, "but it's gonna cost you."

"At this point any price seems reasonable. Will it involve an exchange of body fluids?"

"Mary Agnes, you know I'm saving myself for my bride, speaking of which, I might have just seen her."

"Yeah, I'm saving myself for the next guy with a cute tight butt that comes my way, but to each his own. What is it that you want?"

I took one of the punch cups and guided Mary Agnes to the back of the ball room. I filled the cup with Colonel Lee and handed it to her and she took a sip.

"Jesus Christ, what is this shit?" she asked in a spasm of choking and gasping. "It tastes like anti-freeze."

"It's called Colonel Lee, and I'm sorry if it doesn't meet your usual high standards."

"You need to upgrade your taste in Bourbon. Try something that's been aged in a barrel for a year or two."

"I'll consult you on my future purchase of spirits, but now I need you to give me the inside dope on a certain young lady."

"Point the little bitch out and I'll reveal her deepest secrets," Mary Agnes said as she took another sip from her punch cup, sans the choking and gagging. Colonel Lee was winning her over.

The band had taken a break and we found the girl and her partner standing by the punch bowl talking to some other kids.

"That's her standing over by the punch."

"Well, I'll be damned; it's just like you to pick out the Belle of the Ball. That little number is Lisa Stansell from Sherrod Plantation. Her daddy is probably the second-richest man in the Delta. She is with Bruce Drummond III, aka Trey, whose old man is Bruce Drummond Jr. and just a little richer than Mr. Stansell."

"Where in the hell is Sherrod Plantation?"

"It's in Coahoma County, between Clarksdale and the river."

"Does she go to school in Clarksdale?"

"No way, Jose, she goes to Miss Porter's in Boston. Trey goes to Phillips Exeter in New Hampshire."

"What's wrong, do they have learning disabilities and need special ed?"

"No, you country dumbass, they both go to top-notch prep schools in the east."

"Well, lah de dah for them."

"Everyone expects them to get married, if they can clear it with the SEC and the Justice Department. It would be more of a merger than a marriage."

"Well, you can rest easy on the marriage thing; it ain't gonna happen."

Mary Agnes looked at me with a sly grin and said, "Oh, and why not?"

"Because she's gonna marry me."

"Well, kiss my ass!"

"I told you I was saving myself for Miss Stansell."

I refilled Mary Agnes's punch cup and moved on to work the rest of my plan. The band was playing Honky Tonk and I edged over near the drummer who seemed to be the Red Tops leader. When the number was finished I approached him with my hand extended and said,

"Hi, I'm Tommy Larch and I need a little favor."

He took my hand and shook it saying. "Hi, Tommy Larch, I'm Walter Osborne, how can I help you?"

"I want to spend some time with a certain young lady, but I'm a terrible dancer. It's customary to spend intermission with your last dancing partner; I want that to be me."

"Why don't you just ask her for that dance? They all have a dance card and you can request a certain number."

"That might be a good idea for someone else, but there is no way I'm gonna blow my chances stepping all over her feet. I want to break just before the number ends and thus win intermission by default."

"Sounds like a plan to me. The last number before intermission will be I'm In the Mood for Love. Keep an eye on me and I'll give you the high sign as we begin the last couple of bars. You can make your move if you time it just right."

"Thanks, Walter; you'll never know how much I appreciate this."

"Good Luck, Tommy Larch."

I decided that I needed some fresh air and probably needed to check on the sleeping beauties in the back seat of the car. The night air carried an edge of frost as it tossed the leaves across the parking lot. I looked into the back seat of the Pontiac, and the three party animals were dozing peacefully in the arms of Morpheus, or, more accurately in the embrace of Colonel Lee. They looked good to go for another hour, so I decided not to open Pandora's Box and rouse them from La-La land.

A full moon was rising on the horizon and the lawns and golf course were bathed in a soft yellow glow. This looked like the perfect setting for a walk at intermission. If I got that far, I'd play the rest by ear. In the distance I heard the Red Tops break into the first of I'm In The Mood For Love and headed back to execute my plan.

I found a place on the edge of the dance floor that allowed me to see Walter and keep an eye on Lisa and the creep. He was holding her close and I had to admit, he was a smooth and graceful dancer. I hated him even more. Soon Walter gave me the high sign and I took a deep breath and headed toward the slowly moving couple. I tapped the jerk on the shoulder and grinned as he released his grasp on Lisa and he smiled as I took his place.

I had no more than placed my hand upon her back when the music came to an end.

Okay, Ace, like the dog who caught the damn car, what now?

I decided to go on the offensive and said,

"Hi, my name's Tommy Larch from Cumberland. Would you like to get some punch while we get to know each other?"

"Some punch would be delightful and even better if you had a little bourbon to add some flavor. I've been wondering when you'd make your move."

"That obvious, huh?"

"Just a little; you have hardly taken your eyes off me all evening. By the way, I'm Lisa Stansell."

"That's just the price you pay for being the loveliest creature in the room. I suspect you have grown pretty used to all the male attention, and you can bet I know exactly who you are."

"Did your homework, did you?"

"Actually, I had some assistance; Mary Agnes Barnes is one of my best and oldest friends. She gave me the scoop on you."

"Oh my, an undercover agent as well as bon vivant. I'm impressed with your tactics."

"Well, don't get too invested in my strategy, but I do hope that we will be friends before the evening ends. You know, 'veni, vidi, vinci'.

"I'd say you are two-thirds of the way there, you are definitely here and clearly you've seen; the conquering part may take a little longer."

"On that note of challenge, why don't we go out on the back veranda and marvel at the harvest moon and continue our little get-to-know-you chat?"

"By all means; then we can share some of that half-pint that's in your jacket pocket."

"Miss Stansell, I'd like for you to meet my good friend Colonel Lee, one of the masters of the distiller's art."

"Colonel Lee, is it? Maybe we can have a drink and remove some paint while we're at it."

"I see you are no stranger to the good Colonel."

"We have bootleggers in Coahoma County just like y'all do in Cumberland."

We exited through the French doors from the ball room to the large tile veranda that spanned the back of the Club. The moon had illuminated the putting green and most of the back nine hole of the golf course. I mixed Lisa's punch with a good dollop of whiskey and gave it to her with a slight bow.

We were silently enjoying the moonlit vista, when we were jerked back into the present by a huge commotion taking place near the golf cart shack. There were half a dozen guys in a circle, taunting a solitary figure in the middle. The guy in the middle was Joe Mosely, and it appeared that Joe had finally found his fight. The only problem was that his chief antagonist was about twice his size and had just knocked Joe on his ass.

"Aw shit!" I muttered, and handed Lisa my punch cup, "I can't let this happen. You'll have to excuse me for a minute or two and let me tend to some business."

"The clarion call of battle. No maid can compete when her Southern swain hears the sound of cannon. I'll just hold your drink and await your return, either with your shield or on it."

The big guy was in the process of pounding Joe into a bloody pulp with his buddies egging him on. I have never been saddled with compunction about fighting fair, a concept that always struck me as an oxymoron. I bounded down the brick steps and hit the cart path at full speed. I timed my arrival at the battle site perfectly and slammed into the bully with a forearm to the side of his head. He never saw me coming and this tactic should have taken him out of the fray. All it did was piss him off.

He shook his head a couple of times and a large grin spread across his face. It was clear that this was not his first rodeo and I had aroused an animal instinct that shone in the feral gleam in his eyes. He charged me like a trumpeting bull elephant. My dad had been a Golden Gloves champion in his misspent youth and had always told me "hit 'em in the body, the head is too hard and you can break your hand". That advice rang in my ears as I side-stepped the charging beast and landed a clean right hook to his kidney as he steamed past.

The right hook actually had some effect on him and he paused as he turned to resume his attack. This time he charged right for me, intending to get me in his grasp and squeeze my life away. I lowered into a crouch to meet his charge and catapulted into his chin with the top of my head. He fell like he had been hit with a poleax.

The next thing I know, I am being gang-tackled by his four buddies, and I could feel my feet coming out from under me. Before I could be taken down, two of my assailants dropped away. and I saw Benny out of the corner of my eye kicking both of them into submission. That left me with the other two to deal with, but only one was in my field of vision. I gave him a combination to the gut and he folded over and began to puke.

The last of the punks was having his head used as a speed bag as Trey Drummond cut him to pieces. Trey was clearly a trained and skilled boxer; he would not put this kid away, but seemed intent on beating him to death. Benny and I grabbed Trey and held him immobile. The battle light went out of his eyes and grinning he said,

"Didn't seem fair for you two to have all the fun, so I decided to deal myself a hand. Hope I didn't offend you."

"We are always glad to share the action as well as our booze. Let me fix you a little toddy," I said.

We gathered up Joe and the four of us walked back to the veranda where Lisa was grinning like a donkey chewing briars. She looked at Benny and said, "I know Arthus and Aramis here, you two must be Porthus and D'Artagnan."

105

"Actually, I'm Benny, which is a hell of lot more impressive than some third-rate musketeer."

"I don't count; I got my ass whipped," Joe moaned.

"C'mon, Joe, the guy was twice your size. I thought you were holding your own."

"Yeah, you jumped in just as I had him lulled into a false sense of confidence. I was just about to mount my mighty offensive and bleed all over his tux."

Benny was mixing Trey a bourbon and coke while I reviewed the carnage left in our wake. The five guys were pulling themselves together with a lot of glaring and mumbling, but I doubted that they wanted another dose. The music was just starting and we walked back into the ball room. The balance of the evening passed with the five of us talking, and helping Benny with his half pint of Colonel Lee. I was reconciled to the fact that it would be totally impossible to hate Trey Drummond. In fact, he was a really cool guy and both Benny and I liked him a lot.

Toward the end of the evening Lisa introduced us to her mother, who was a stunning beauty in her own right, and they invited Benny, Joe and I to their home for a dinner party the next Friday night. Lisa let me know that she and Trey were good friends, but had no romantic interest in each other, which was the best news I had received all night. Soon Rufus McKay was crooning Danny Boy and Lisa asked me to dance.

I was in the process of explaining how I didn't have a clue how to dance when she grabbed my hand and pulled me close to her. Before I knew it I was dancing, or at least swaying with the music and experiencing as much heaven on earth as I have ever enjoyed. Too soon she and Trey were joining her mother and their driver to head back home. I watched their taillights fade out of sight and abruptly returned to reality.

The reality was pretty grim; the three sleeping beauties had awakened sometime in the second half of the dance and had begun working on what was left of the fifth of Early Times. By the time we found them they were all tuned up and ready to party.

"Goddamn, where the hell y'all been, you missed our little backseat cocktail party. This is the best dance I've ever been to," gushed Hogan.

"Jimmy, the dance is over, it's one o'clock in the morning and time we headed home," I said.

"Hell, it's too early to go home, let's go to the whorehouse in Vicksburg and get some strange."

"Hell, Hogan, anything other than your right hand would be strange to you. We ain't going to Vicksburg, or anywhere other than Cumberland. Get your ass in the car and let's go."

"Man, you guys are a bunch of pussies; just when we get ready to rock and roll you want to go home."

The other two were nodding their agreement and encouraging Hogan's attempts to keep the party going. Finally, Benny had enough and very calmly said, "If you three assholes don't get your sorry butts in the backseat of this car, I'm going to rip your heads off and shit in your necks."

The three of them knew Benny was no longer joking but was completely ready to carry out his threat. They meekly got in the back of the car and before we were out of Rosedale, they had gone back to sleep.

"What the hell are we going to do when we get back to town? We can't drop Hogan at his house and keep his car overnight. We'll have to sober him up enough for him to at least drive himself home."

"I guess we can take them to the C&P and try to get some coffee down him."

The C&P was a truck stop on the edge of Cumberland that stayed open all night. We usually ate breakfast there when we were going duck hunting. The C&P Café was locally known as the Choke & Puke. It was hard to screw up breakfast, but the C&P could do it.

We herded the three campers into a booth and ordered six cups of coffee. The waitress delivered the coffee and Joe took a long gulp.

"Shit, this is worse than the coffee we get a Guard camp; it tastes like battery acid."

"We're talking medicinal effect, not flavor, here," I said. "Just see if you can get a couple of cups down our trio of zombies."

It took about an hour, but we finally had three badly hung over but nearly sober young men. I drove everyone home and pulled up in front of my house, before I let Hogan touch the steering wheel. I checked and made sure he was fully awake and set him off on his four-block journey home. That's when I noticed the lights on in our living room.

Oh my God, I don't want to have to rehash the whole evening with Miss Manners, but I can't very well sneak in without her seeing me, or could I? I eased around to the back of our house and climbed up on the dog house that was just under my bedroom window. Napoleon, my twelve–year-old mongrel was sleeping off his big dish of dog food and never heard me. Napoleon was not the dog he once was. I quietly raised my window and swung my leg into the room as I heard a ripping sound of fabric being torn.

Oh shit! I made it through two bottles of Colonel Lee, a dance and a gang fight without destroying my new tux only to ruin it getting to bed. What the hell, Ike will be able to fix it. He was, after all, a master tailor, plus, he had an economic interest in the suit. I bet he can have it ready by next week's dance in Greenwood. I guess I better find out what the well-dressed prep schooler would wear to a dinner invitation as well, maybe Ike would extend some more credit.

Pretty soon I was deep in dreamland walking through the woods with Miss Lisa Stansell on my arm and joy in my heart.

Bombs Away

"Where in the hell are you going at nine o'clock at night?" Dad asked as I slipped on my heavy jacket and grabbed my car keys from their hook by the kitchen door.

"Gonna pick up Benny and ride out to the El Rancho to see what's happening. I'll be home about eleven or so."

"You boys be careful," added Mom. This was her standard comment when one of her children departed. I could have been about to exit the landing craft onto Omaha Beach and she would have said the same thing.

I stepped into the winter night and the cold nearly took my breath away.

Good Lord, its cold as a well digger's ass in Wyoming. Wish I had warmed up my car.

I started the car and turned the heater to full blast. I left the engine idling, opened the trunk and began to scrounge around in my box of hunting gear. I found my leather gloves and my wool watch hat and pulled them on. I took a quick check of the one hundred feet of steel tow chain just to be sure it was still there. Good, I was ready to go.

The heater had begun to warm things up a bit, so I turned it down a notch and flipped on the defroster. We needed to have maximum visibility tonight. I drove the three blocks to Benny's house and pulled into his driveway. Again I left my car idling and knocked on his back door. Benny's dad came to the door, sporting his standard scowl, and groaned, "Oh, it's you," turned and left me standing in the doorway.

Who the hell was he expecting, Winston Churchill?

I realized that I was not Mr. Bowman's favorite person; in fact he would be happier if Benny was hanging around with Vlad the Impaler. Too bad Vlad wasn't available. I walked in and went to Benny's room.

He was getting his winter gear on as we went out a side door into his garage. Benny was a tinkerer and a modeler, and his Dad had built a mini workshop in one of the storerooms off the garage. Benny opened a cabinet and pulled out a black object that looked like a cross between a football and a bowling ball. This was "Big Boy," which he carefully put in a gym bag as we slipped out to the driveway. Benny gently placed "Big Boy" on the floor of the passenger side as we eased out of the drive onto the street.

Benny and I had been blowing things up since we first discovered M80's and Cherry Bombs at about the age of six. We recently ordered a twenty-five pound canister of black powder from an ad in *Argosy Magazine*. A fair amount of that powder was tucked inside "Big Boy". Benny was a natural bomb maker and for tonight's mission he had outdone himself.

Starting with a tennis ball can filled with black powder, he wrapped six full rolls of athletic tape securely around the entire package. He then drilled a hole through to the powder. Just prior to detonation he would insert two and a half feet of glass capillary tubing into the hole. The tubing was filled with black powder and would burn at one foot per minute. We would have two minutes and thirty seconds to do the deal. When he finished he used shoe polish to dye the whole thing black. I drove away feeling like Col. Tibbets must have felt as the Enola Gay cleared the runway.

"You ready to do this?" I asked.

"You bet, we're locked and loaded; let's do it." Benny replied.

"Damn right, we'll strike a blow against tyranny and get a little revenge at the same time."

The reign of tyranny led directly to Cumberland's new Chief of Police. He had been hired late last summer after an undistinguished career in Dayton, Ohio. The City Fathers, in their infinite wisdom decided that now that Cumberland had a total of five full-time policemen, they would surely need an experienced leader. They picked the current bozo for reasons that were unfathomable to us. He was a real jerk, and more to the point, he was a damn Yankee.

Under the old system there was an unspoken truce between the teenagers of Cumberland and the cops. They knew all of us by sight and knew all of our parents. They coached us in sports and were part of our daily lives. Unless there was a violent felony involved, they made every effort to let us slide. They rarely passed out traffic tickets and turned a blind eye to most of our pranks. They were good guys and we liked them.

Then Genghis Khan came on the scene. Benny and I had been handed a total of eleven traffic tickets since school began. This was humiliating and grossly unfair, not to mention damned expensive. Not one of the tickets had been issued for a serious offense. Minor speeding in school zones for instance. Fifty-five Mph should be well within the parameters of acceptance if you're late for football practice. Jesse Carr had been caught doing 115 Mph between Abbeville and Cumberland; now that was worth a ticket. A couple of Hollywood stops and driving outside the lines should have been ignored, and it would have been under the previous regime. This could not go unpunished. That punishment fell to the two most experienced and prepared operatives in Cumberland; Benny and me.

We were very experienced in covert operations. We had been pulling off pranks of one kind or another since we were first allowed to leave home unattended. We had managed to do this without getting caught, with the notable exception of Benny's somewhat amateurish attempt to rob the U.S. Mail when he was seven. I will always believe that if Benny had not jumped off the reservation and tried to do a one-man show, we could have handled the Feds as well. Benny was absolutely fearless and would try anything, but I bring a sound planning element to our work, and he should have consulted me before trying to steal the mail. The U.S. Mail Inspectors, accompanied by a U.S. Marshall, had cracked the case within 30 days of Benny's first mail theft. The fact that he kept the unopened letters in his room may have helped the government's sleuths as they detected. His summary conviction was followed by having to spend most of the summer in his own yard. This was before ankle bracelets, and he violated his parole on most days. We had the necessary experience.

We also had extensive military training. When E Company, Second Battalion of the 155th Infantry Regiment, Mississippi National Guard, had returned from Korea in 1953, they had been decimated by two years of hard combat and the return to civilian life of many of the rank and file. They would accept anyone dumb enough to join. Benny and I lied about our ages, gained our parents' permission and became fourteen-year old infantryman. The past two summers we had attended infantry training at Fort McClellan, Alabama, and considered ourselves lean, mean, killing machines. We were experienced, trained, and boy, were we motivated; we hated Genghis Khan's guts. All of this was coming together on this frigid, overcast December night. The plan had been carefully tested. We knew our roles and we had our timing down pat. The fog of war was our only concern. As we passed the Cumberland State Bank the temperature was 22°F.

I drove to the north end of the alley that ran behind the police station, pulled into a parking place, cut the lights and left the engine running. Benny and I exchanged places and he moved behind the wheel. The first phase of our plan put me in the action role. Benny kicked the defroster up to high, turned on the headlights and we began to move south.

We approached the rear of the police station and Benny eased to a stop, leaving the engine running. I slipped out of the passenger side and opened the trunk. I hefted the plastic box holding the tow chain out of the trunk and closed the lid as quietly as possible. Benny drove off as I moved stealthily between the police station and the adjacent building, staying in the shadows. Once in position, I could see the police cars lined up just like the fighters on Clark Field, totally unprepared.

The Chief got the goodies: a brand new Ford Crown Victoria with a special police package V8 engine and his very own parking place. I struggled the box of chain in position between the Chief's new car and a city fire hydrant about ten feet behind it. One hundred feet of heavy duty towing chain weighs about ninety pounds. I scored the double-hooked chain from Jesse Carr. I had been Jesse's freshman rookie on the football team and he treated me like a little brother. I didn't ask him where he got the chain, and he

113

didn't tell. He did assure me that it would not be traceable back to either of us. Forensic science was in its infancy.

The mercury vapor lamps that had just been installed along Main Street lit up the night, and I knew I had to work fast to avoid detection. I hooked one end of the chain to the fire hydrant and crawled under the back of the Chief's car, attached the other end to the back axle. There was still about eighty feet of slack chain in the box. I eased out from under the car and slipped between the buildings back to the alley. I could see Benny and the car idling at the North end of the alley. I waved and he started toward me. I jumped into the driver's seat as Benny slid over.

"How'd it go?" he asked.

"Like a Swiss watch so far," I replied as I eased down the alley. "Now you're on."

"Well don't you fret, Benny the bomber is on the case."

I have to admit I was not fretting, Benny was to homemade bombs as Ted Williams was to hitting a baseball, the best there was. We began executing the second phase of our plan. I drove back to the north end of the alley and watched for the stop light at the south end to turn red. When it did, I moved down the alley at 15 miles per hour and came to a stop behind the police station. Benny picked up "Big Boy" and slipped out of the car. He opened the lid of the big green dumpster that rested against the back wall of the station, inserted the device and lit the fuse before closing the lid. "Big Boy" had been launched.

The self imposed rules of engagement under which we operated required that no injury be inflicted and collateral material damage be held to a minimum. We were certain that the steel dumpster would give us an extra margin of safety. The endgame of this operation would be to see the Chief dash to his cruiser and race away in pursuit of the perps that caused the blast. He should get about 80 feet before his rear end disengaged itself from the rest of his car. Everybody would get a big laugh at his expense, and maybe he'd decide that he needed to go back to Dayton; just a boyish prank.

We hit the south end of the alley right on schedule and took a right on Court Street. We had timed the blast to take place when we were about a half-mile on the other side of town. With the windows up to keep out the cold, we would probably not be able to hear the detonation, but we were confident that by the time we returned downtown it would all be over. I had just made the turn at the end of Court and started back downtown when the entire sky in front of us erupted in a flash of light. The flash was followed by a deafening sound and a shock wave that actually rocked the car. We fully expected to see a huge mushroom cloud on the horizon.

"Oh my God!" Benny exclaimed, "We killed them all."

"Don't panic; let's just see how bad it is."

"I'm not sure I really want to know how bad it is. You might just drop me by my house on your way downtown and fill me in later."

"No way, Jose, we'll go down together. We've worked our way out of worse situations than this."

"Name one."

"I'll get back to you on that."

I drove at a steady 30 Mph and reached the intersection of Court and Main in about a minute and a half. We looked toward the police station and were greeted with a scene straight out of the movies. The police station was missing its back end. There was no sign of the dumpster, but I did happen to notice the green steel lid sitting atop one of the totaled police cruisers. The Chief was standing by what remained of his new car. The rear end was not in sight and the Chief had that thousand-yard stare associated with close quarter combat.

There was a 150-foot geyser of water pumping into the cold night air from the stump of the missing fire hydrant. The steel tow chain had done its job. It ripped the rear axle and differential completely out of the Chief's car. It also ripped the fire hydrant out of the ground like a bad wisdom tooth. The spewing water was covering everything within a two-block area with a thick coat of ice. There were no first responders on the scene, and Benny and I decided we would only get in the way. It was time for us to go home.

The next morning at breakfast my Dad had been reading the Memphis Commercial Appeal which provided us with our daily news. The TV was on the Today Show and neither mentioned the mayhem in downtown Cumberland. I thought it best to let sleeping dogs lie and left to go get Benny.

Benny got in the car as if in slow motion as I asked,

"How'd you sleep?"

"Like a baby." He said, "I would sleep a while and wake up and cry awhile, how 'bout you?"

"About the same. I got up and made a list of things I needed to do before they sentence us. Twenty years seems like a reasonable time to serve. Of course this is your second felony; they may throw the book at you."

"Whatever, it doesn't make much difference, my old man's going to kill me anyway."

"I'm kinda hoping we might get away with the Marine Corps plea bargain. Paris Island ain't so bad."

"The French Foreign Legion is probably a better bet. They have an office in New Orleans and they don't ask any questions. We could be there by mid afternoon and be gone to Algeria or Diem Bien Phu by tomorrow."

"Let's don't lose our guts yet; we really don't know the lay of the land. Why don't we ease by Katz's Pool Hall and check on the latest rumors."

"Good idea, I could use a strong cup of coffee."

We had to drive right by the still smoldering ruins of the police station to get to Katz. At least they had managed to cut the fire hydrant off, but there was a thick coating of ice on the wrecked police cars. There was a wrecker loading the remains of the Chief's car on to a flat bed truck. It looked like it was totaled to me. There was no sign of Genghis Khan.

We walked into Katz's and took a seat at the counter. Archie Dalton was working the first shift and came over to get our order.

"What in the hell is going on across the street?" I asked with as much innocence as I could muster.

"You mean y'all haven't heard? Those damn gypsies blew up the police station last night."

"You mean Ramon and his tribe, the ones that always winter at the fairgrounds?"

"Yeah, they're gone this morning, cleared out in the middle of the night."

"Why would Ramon blow up our police station? I thought we had a deal with those guys. Our cops wouldn't hassle them, and they wouldn't steal from the locals. They've been here every winter since I can remember."

"Yeah, well that was working just fine, until that asshole of a new Chief decided Ramon and his folks were not a civic asset and started to constantly jack them around. I guess he found out what happens when you screw with the Romanis. He got his ass fired this morning as soon as the Mayor found out the deal. He will be long gone when he is released from the hospital in Greenville where he seems to be in a state of shock."

"Gypsies, huh? Well you never know who you can mess with. C'mon, Benny, let's go duck hunting.

Weekend Warriors

The morning sky was just starting to hint at the oncoming dawn, the faintest pink tinge to the receding purple night. It was a quarter to five when Benny and I pulled into the armory parking lot. We unloaded our duffel bags, hiked them over our shoulders and started looking for the second platoon assembly area. We spotted Sgt. Jesse Carr, our platoon sergeant. He saw us coming and said,

"I'm glad you girls could join us this morning. I hope it didn't cause y'all any inconvenience."

"As a matter of fact it did. I had plans to sleep till noon and spend the rest of the day at the pool," I replied.

"I'm afraid that it couldn't be avoided, Uncle Sam wants you!"

"It'll be worth it, knowing that the civilian population will be able to sleep tonight because we're manning the walls against the red commie hordes."

"Your National Guard is ever on the alert," Benny threw in.

"Pile your personal gear over there and go help load the weapons." Jesse ordered. "We are pulling out at 5:30 sharp, and Cap'n Millstone will probably keelhaul anyone that holds us up. It damn sure won't be second platoon."

It was mid-July in the Mississippi Delta and the morning air had cooled to a chilly 88F and a hardly noticeable 90% humidity. We began to help the rest of the platoon load up our weapons. There were three rifle squads of two NCO's with eight men each. Each squad was responsible for eight M-1 rifles, one Browning Automatic Rifle, affectionately known as a BAR, two .45 Colt Automatic pistols and two M-2 Carbines. The fourth squad in a rifle platoon was the weapons squad.

The weapons squad had two sections of three men and one NCO. There was a Browning .30 cal. air-cooled machine gun section and a 60mm mortar section. A sergeant was squad leader and two corporals led the two sections. Benny and I were in the machine gun section. I fired the weapon and carried the receiver and barrel while Benny fed the belts of ammunition and carried the big tripod. The third guy carried the ammo, and the corporal's job was to stay on our ass.

A rifle company had three rifle platoons of forty men each, a weapons platoon of an additional forty men and a headquarters platoon of forty men, administrative NCOs, clerks, medics, cooks and quite a few generally useless ass-kissers. We walked, they rode. They were quaintly known as REMF's or Rear Echelon Mother F**kers. That all added up to 160 men and officers at full strength. We were close to fully staffed.

By the time we loaded all of the weapons and our personal gear, the sun was peeking over the trees on the adjacent municipal golf course and we were sweating through our olive drab fatigues. A whistle blew and First Sergeant Pauli Maggio had us fall in company formation. After the Platoon sergeants reported that all their men were present and accounted for, the First Sergeant turned to Captain James Millstone and shouted,

"E Company, Second Battalion, 155th Infantry Regiment all present or accounted for, SIR!"

Captain James H. Millstone stood ramrod straight. He was wearing crisply starched, sharply creased olive green fatigues. His paratrooper boots were gleaming in the early morning light which reflected off his silver Captain's bars and the brass crossed rifles of the infantry. There were no ribbons or decorations on the left breast of his uniform, just the wings of a paratrooper with three combat jumps and the blue of the combat infantry badge with three stars. Millstone commanded respect and the men of Easy Company would have followed him anywhere.

"AT EASE!" Millstone shouted. "Now, listen up. Today, we are going to execute the most dangerous peacetime maneuver that an Infantry unit can undertake. We are going to move a regiment of men across two states in the next 24 hours. One regiment, four battalions, twenty companies or approximately 3500 officers and men.

We will be joined by three additional regiments, the 167th Infantry of the Alabama National Guard, 187th Infantry of the Florida National Guard and the 114th Artillery Regiment. These units are the fighting components of the 31st Infantry Division, the Dixie Division. A total of close to 15,000 officers and men.

I am in command of the combined convoys of the 155th. In the past there have been several deaths due to avoidable accidents when the 155th attempted this maneuver this year there will be none. I will turn over the command of Easy Company to First Lieutenant Jerry Young, our Executive Officer, and I will assume command of the 114th Military Police Company. I expect that every Officer and NCO in Easy Company will assume a personal responsibility to get our men safely to Fort McClellan. That is all. Load up and move out."

The First Sergeant dismissed the formation and we all headed for our 2.5 ton trucks, referred to as "deuce-and-a-half's". Each of the big trucks would hold twenty men seated on fold down benches lining both sides of the rear section of the truck. All of their gear and weapons would be stowed in the area between the benches.

The trucks were painted a matte olive drab with white lettering on the front bumpers that said: Co.E 2nd Bat. 155th Inf. Each had a olive drab canvas top that could be secured in case of bad weather, but today the trucks would start out with the sides rolled open. It was too damn hot to be closed up. Easy Company had eight deuce-and-a-half's. The balance of the company would be riding in four large weapons carriers and a half dozen jeeps.

The convoy would stretch for a half mile with the road guards racing ahead and controlling traffic at intersections. We expected to average 35 miles per hour with stops along the way for piss calls and noon chow. Our first day's objective was Columbus, Mississippi, ten miles from the Alabama state line.

We pulled out of Cumberland with a police escort to the Sunflower County line and we were all in good spirits. Benny and I had grabbed the last two seats near the back of our truck with the wind helping to cool the advancing heat of mid-morning. This would be our third summer camp at Fort McClellan and we felt like seasoned veterans. We had joined the Guard when they returned from the Korean War and were desperate for bodies. Our parents lied about our age, we were 14 at the time, and everybody turned a blind eye as we became ninth-grade infantry men. We would soon be seniors in high school, and both of us would be up for Corporal when we finished this year's training. This should be our last year for KP, latrine duty and garbage details.

It took about an hour to reach Highway 82 at Moorhead. Our convoy pulled to the side of the road and made way for D Company joining us from Indianola. Benny looked at the trucks of Dog Company as they assumed the convoy lead and said,

"It really makes no sense for those yahoos from Indianola to get ahead of us. We are clearly the sharper outfit."

"If you'll remind me, I'll bring that up the next time Cap'n Millstone and I get together to discuss convoy tactics," I replied.

"Yeah, see what you can do. While you're at it, you might mention what a jack-off that fat slug Corolla is. He should be busted to buck-assed private."

"O.K., I'll work on it. In the meantime that'll be Sergeant Corolla to you, and for the next two weeks he is your Lord and Master."

Anthony Corolla was a member of the Shaw mafia. A group of inter-married Italian farmers that seemed to gain high rank among the non commissioned officers of Easy Company. First Sergeant Pauli Maggio was the titular leader of the club. He and Millstone had served together in the 101st Airborne in WWII, and he looked after his extended family. The only WASP holding rank above E-5 was our platoon sergeant Jesse Carr. Jesse was a Sergeant First Class, that's three up and two down. Jesse was a born leader and reluctantly accepted by the mafia.

As the larger convoy resumed its crawl across Mississippi, the talk among the troops began to fade into a heat-induced quiet. The deuce-and-a-half is a sturdily built, heavy duty vehicle. It was built for reliability and performance and can withstand terrible amounts of punishment and abuse. It was not built for comfort. I always suspect that the suspension system was left out as just something else to break-down. It was a rough-riding mother. Every expansion joint in the highway sent a sharp shockwave right up your ass. The nicest thing that you could say about a deuce-and-a-half is that it beat the hell out of walking and toting.

The trucks droned out a steady beat as we moved across the dark green landscape of the Delta. Cotton, soybeans and rice fields stretched to the horizon on all sides. The rhythmic cadence soon reduced us to a sun-dulled stupor. Heads were nodding and the rasp of open-mouthed snoring lent a counterpoint to the roaring sound of mud grip tires on pavement.

Everyone began to stir when the convoy turned north at Winona and headed for the chow call scheduled at Camp McCain, just outside of Duck Hill. Camp McCain was the Mississippi National Guard's firing range. We came one weekend a year, bivouacked (read camped out) and used the firing range to qualify with our personal weapons. When not used, the military reservation was closed and shuttered. Today it was to be the site of our noon break .

Each Company's cooks had pulled out at midnight to give them time to set up their field kitchens and provide a hot meal for the convoys. We pulled into Easy Company's parking area and the smell of fried chicken filled the air. It is said that an Army moves on its stomach and Cap'n Millstone was a firm believer. The regular army chow was pretty darn good and there was always plenty of it. I have to admit that I liked it all, including creamed chipped beef on toast (shit on a shingle) and Spam.

Easy Company maintained a food fund that was used to supplement the regular rations issued by the Army. We ate very well. After a quick formation to make sure we hadn't lost anyone so far, we lined up to eat. Benny and I were both chow hounds, and we made it to the first third of the line. The sooner you got your food, the longer the after-chow naps.

We passed through the serving line and the cooks piled our mess kits high with fried chicken, mashed potatoes, gravy, green beans, sliced bread and jello. We filled our canteen cups with iced tea and sat down in the shade of our truck to eat.

"You know, in spite of being sloppy, lazy and alcoholic, our cooks turn out some pretty tasty stuff," Benny said.

"The only reason is that Millstone eats with us and not in the officer's mess. They're scared to death he'll make them riflemen and set the fat asses to walking. If they keep the quality of the chow up, he lets them slide on most everything else." I replied.

It was a fact, Millstone and all of our officers ate with the men when we were in the field. They would wait until every man had gone through the chow line before they would be served. When we were on base they would take turns eating in our mess hall. We never ate a meal without an officer sharing it. Like I said, the food was pretty darn good.

Benny and I finished our food and walked over to the large water barrel heated to almost boiling by a kerosene fueled immersion heater. We scraped off any excess food, used a brush in the hot water to clean the gear and then dipped them in another barrel of clean steaming water to rinse the soap off. You only need to get diarrhea once from an unclean mess kit to learn to do this right.

We put our mess kits away and picked a choice spot under the truck to grab a nap. We used our helmet liners as pillows and were soon snoring away. If you have been around the military for any length of time you quickly realize that you never know the next time you will be able to sleep, so take advantage of every opportunity. The same goes for eating and bodily functions. The convoy is not going to stop at the next Shell station for you to use the john.

We were awakened by Sgt. Maggio's shrill whistle and the scream " FALL IN!" We held another quick head count to make sure no one had wandered off. We were given fifteen minutes to make a latrine call and be back on the trucks. We were soon back on the road with most of us were continuing our after-chow naps.

Two more First Battalion Companies joined us at McCain, and we picked up the two remaining companies of the Second Battalion when we passed back through Winona. The Third Battalion would meet us tonight in Columbus. The convoy now stretched for over two miles in total length. We ground along at 35 Mph as the afternoon wore on.

By four in the afternoon we were stopped on the outskirts of Starkville where the last of the First Battalion joined up, and we began to move down the highway on the last twenty five miles of the day's march. We passed through downtown Columbus, Mississippi, home of Mississippi State College for Women, or as we all called it, the "W". Summer school was still in session and several hundred coeds lined the wrought iron fence as we crept by accompanied with hoots and hollers from nearly a thousand horny young men.

"Benny looked at the gaggle of coeds and said, "Now that's a target-rich environment if ever I saw one."

"It is that for sure; this time next year we'll be spending a good bit of our time over here."

Benny and I were planning on going to Mississippi State College in Starkville, just twenty-five miles west, and the W would be our happy hunting ground.

The convoy continued to the eastern outskirts of Columbus to a large fairgrounds area known as Probst Park. The convoy snaked through the park with units peeling off at their assigned bivouac areas. We joined the rest of 2nd Battalion in a large grassy area close to Highway 82. We dismounted and fell in for another formation. We were still all in attendance. 1st Lt. Young called the formation to at ease and gave us the scoop.

"Okay, listen up. The platoon sergeants will stake out each platoon's area and you will pitch your shelter halves and ditch 'em. It is not scheduled to rain, but you never know. Once your squad leaders have inspected your tents and gear, we will fall back in before you go through the chow line. Any questions?" Now trust me on this. "Any questions?" was a purely rhetorical question; you

125

would rather poke a tiger in the eye than ask an officer a dumb question.

Sgt. Carr inspected our area, pronounced it passable and we were called back into formation. Sgt. Maggio assigned the night duty to each platoon. Second platoon drew guard duty. It could have been worse; we had avoided latrine and KP, short for kitchen police. Maggio continued on with the scoop; if you did not draw a night duty assignment you would be free to go into Columbus and see the sights." This translated into going to the W or one of the several dozen beer joints that lined Hwy 82 across the Tombigbee River.

Since neither Benny nor I were doing much drinking as we prepared for the start of fall football practice in August, we decided to volunteer for guard duty if we could wrangle an IOU out of Sgt. Carr. I tracked Jesse down near the Company headquarters tent and ask permission to speak.

"Permission granted," he said. "What's on your mind?"

"Well, you know August 15th is getting near, and Benny and I can't do much drinking, so we thought we would volunteer for guard duty tonight and let some other guys go into town. Maybe we can avoid some little minor duty later on when we get to McClellan."

"A quid pro quo, huh?" he said with a grin.

"Something like that."

"What did I tell you about volunteering for anything? Don't you even hear me when I'm talking to you?"

Jesse had played center on the Cumberland High football team when Benny and I first turned out. I had been his rookie for two years and we had a close relationship. I'm beginning to wonder if we had screwed up.

I said, "I actually didn't volunteer, I sorta floated the idea by you. I can always withdraw it."

126

"Too late for that. You eager young troopers will indeed serve on guard duty tonight, and for the next two weeks I'll know where to find "volunteers" when I need them. Report to the Officer of the Day in fifteen minutes with full combat gear and your weapons."

Benny, who had been standing just behind me, said, "Now, that went well didn't it?"

"Yeah, wonder why I have the feeling that we just screwed up?"

Benny and I saddled up with full combat gear, including steel helmets, and reported to the Officer of the Day, some 2nd Lt. from Meadville. He was assigning guard post and gave Benny Post 23 and I got Post 24. There was a Cpl. driving a three-quarter-ton weapons carrier to take us to our appointed post. We soon realized that 23 and 24 were the end of the road. All of the other guards were taking post like the center field fence of a ball diamond or a picnic area with benches and cover.

The weapons carrier turned down a small dirt road with woods crowding in on all sides. The headlights just revealed more dirt road and more trees. About a quarter of a mile into the woods the road took a steep nose over into a hardwood bottom. Soon he stopped and Benny got out with the assurance that he should walk through the woods until he came to the river. I was put out about 200 yards further along with the same instruction.

The weapons carrier ground out a 180 and soon its tail lights disappeared from view. It occurred to me that this was very much like being dumped on your deer stand before daylight. I decided to treat this like a hunting trip and positioned myself against a huge oak tree facing the fast moving Tombigbee. If you enter the woods with a bunch of noise and rattling around, it will take a few minutes for the natural rhythm of nature to resume.

I quietly leaned against my tree and let my breathing return to normal. Soon the sounds of the woods and night picked up around me. The hoot of an owl echoed from across the river and the scampering rustle of night critters rose from the undergrowth. Things were peaceful and serene.

I have never understood exactly how stinging insects can coordinate their attacks with such precision. For the first five minutes or so everything was fine. The sun was long gone and the woods were bathed in a bright moonlit twilight. As if someone had sent a signal, every mosquito in the Tombigbee River bottom swarmed my exposed skin. I slapped, I cursed and I danced a jig. I was worried that I would soon pass out from the tremendous loss of blood that was being sucked out of my pierced extremities.

I heard Benny trashing around downstream apparently facing the same assault. I thought longingly of the six cans of OFF! that were nestled in my duffel bag, hell of a lot of good it was doing me now. It's a funny thing about mosquitoes, if you resist, they will carry your ass off, but if you relax and stop swatting and slapping they will settle down to a slow but steady theft of your vital fluids. I had learned that hunting turkeys in the Spring and shooting ducks with my grandfather in South Louisiana. Just ignore the little bastards and they will soon lose interest.

I was determined to sit as quietly as possible and allow the woods to regain their rhythm. Soon all was serene again. The full moon reflected off the slowly moving river and hundreds of sparkling ripples danced in the turgid current. The owl across the river was hooting away and all of God's little creatures were busy doing their nightly thing. Guard duty consisted of two four- hour shifts and we were slated to be replaced at 11 pm. We had about an hour and a half to go.

The still night was shattered by the clear sound of three loud shotgun blasts in the far distance and there was soon the baying of a pack of beagles hot on the trail of something.

Must be some coon hunters running their dogs in the thick swamp across the river, I thought.

This was cool; I loved to hear a pack of hounds working their quarry. We still hunted deer with dogs and you quickly learned to follow the race to be sure you saw the deer if it came your way. I could tell from the growing sound of the pack that whatever they were chasing was headed for the river. We might catch a sight of a deer or maybe a black bear swimming to our bank.

Now I not only could hear the dogs closing in on the far side of the river, but I could hear the sapling-busting sound of a very large mammal crashing through the underbrush. Far in the distance I could hear human voices shouting as they drove the dogs. It appeared that Benny and I were going to have a ringside seat to the climax of the chase.

The crashing across the river intensified and I figured that a big buck was going to break cover and plunge in the river. Instead, a large ape like figure came crashing into the river and started swimming frantically toward me. By this time the dogs had reached the bank as well and were milling about, unsure of their next move. The dark figure in the water had just set a world free-style record for fifty meters and was dragging itself to shore. I could now see that it was a man.

"HALT, WHO GOES THERE!" I shouted, just as we had been trained to do. The dark figure looked up in stark amazement, apparently speechless.

"ADVANCE AND BE RECOGNIZED!" I yelled, again.

The man just stared at me as if he was seeing a spook. "LISTEN, YOU DUMBASS, I HAVE AN M-1 RIFLE AIMED AT YOUR STUPID HEAD. ADVANCE AND BE RECOGNIZED!" I screamed just a little rattled. It was true, I had my M-1 zeroed in on his head, and the fact that we were not issued any ammunition seemed a minor point at the time.

I was beginning to get a little nervous, I had exhausted everything that I had been trained to do and the jerk still had not responded to me. I decided that the absence of ammo would not keep me from defending my post. If necessary, I would use the M-1 as a club in the upcoming hand-to-hand combat. Then I realized that I was carrying the bayonet for the M-1, and I hastily begin to click it in place and mount what would have probably been the last bayonet charge of the U.S. Army. Before I could get the bayonet in place, the guy looked at me and said, "Larch, is that you?"

Completely taken aback, I meekly said, "Yeah, it's me. Who in the hell are you?"

The figure came climbing up the bank as I warily covered him with my now mounted bayonet.

"It's me, dummy, George Bines."

If your system has just received a large jolt of adrenalin it tends to sharpen your senses, but it can adversely affect your ability to reason. I knew that Georg Bines was a friend of mine. George was in a different platoon than Benny and me, and he had been the fullback on last year's football team. Of course I knew him, I just couldn't find the right words.

He drug himself up the bank and sat down against my tree. The dogs across the river continued to make the "we've got him treed" sounds and they were soon joined by four shotgun-toting locals flashing high powered hand lanterns. They swept the bank on our side of the river with their lanterns and pinpointed me in the glare.

"Hey, boy," they said, "you seen the sumbitch my dog's been chasin' ?"

Next to calling me "Red", nothing pissed me off more than calling me "boy".

"Naw," I called out. "Nobody came this way. Your dogs are probably all turned around,"

There's nothing, short of cussin' his mama, that will piss a redneck off like suggesting that his dogs aren't on top of their game. At this point everybody is pissed off.

"Goddamn, boy, you disrespect my dogs and I gonna swim this f**king river and whip yo' ass."

"Well, Billy Bob, just dive on in and drag your shit-kicking country ass over here and we'll see who gets whipped."

"Why don't I just load your ass up with some number four shot and skip the swim," he called back.

"Well, for one reason I don't think you want to start a gunfight with two dudes carrying M-1s. I'll plant a round of .30 caliber ball ammunition right between your pig-faced eyes. How's that grab you?" I said and held my rifle up for emphasis.

There was a couple of moments of muttering consultation among the posse across the river, then Billy Bob shouted back, "This thing ain't over, by God!" and they gathered up their dogs and walked away.

By the time they were out of sight Benny strolled up from his post downstream and said, "Nicely done, for a man without a single round of .30 caliber ball ammunition. You ran a pretty good bluff."

"I was so damn mad I would have stuck this bayonet up his redneck ass along with that piece of shit shotgun. Son-of-a-bitch called me boy."

"Yeah, I heard him do it not once, but twice, at least he didn't call you 'Red'."

"It's a damn good thing he didn't , I would've probably swum that river and yanked his head off and shit in his neck."

"That'd get his attention." Benny said, as he turned to George who was finally getting his wind back, and asked, "Bines, there is undoubtedly a story surrounding your recent narrow escape from the hounds of hell."

"Actually, it was all a big misunderstanding. I was tarred with the brush of association by Fenton and Willis. I was really an innocent bystander."

"How did Fenton and Willis manage to make you beagle bait?" I asked.

"It all started as a quiet, boring evening in downtown Columbus. The three of us caught the deuce-and-a-half delivering guys to the W and downtown just to see the local sights. There is absolutely nothing in downtown Columbus after dark, so we decided to go across the river to some of the tonks and check them out."

"My bet is that there ain't much happening in downtown Columbus at any time of day," mused Benny.

"Probably not, but there ain't a hell'uv lot goin' on in the tonks either. You can drink some beer, shoot some pool and do a little recreational fighting with the airmen from Columbus Air Force Base and the local loggers. That's about it."

"I'd pick the Air Force pussies if I needed to start a fight. One logger is worth six blue pukes," I said.

"We didn't even start a fight. Fenton was playing the pinball machine, you know they pay-off over here, and got a little exuberant trying to steer the ball. The machine tilted and he gave it a righteous kick that broke one of the front legs. The machine collapsed and started making a real spectacle of itself. Every light was flashing, every bell was dinging and it started to rack up about a hundred points. Finally, I reached over and unplugged the damn thing about the time one of the bouncers came charging over."

"I take it he took offense at Fenton's abuse of the fixtures?" Benny asked.

"It's safe to say that Fenton and the bouncer had differing ideas on what should happen next. The bouncer was in favor of the three of us paying for the machine, and Fenton wanted to cash in the several hundred points that had been racked up in the carnage. Their debate was beginning to get pretty heated. When I made the mistake of suggesting that the games that Fenton had scored should more than cover the damages, and let's just call it even."

"George, that was a very mature response to a delicate situation. Did the parties agree to your mediation?"

"Not exactly, Fenton got pissed at me and told me to keep my f**king mouth out of his personal business and the bouncer ask me how I'd like my ass kicked?"

"I hesitate to ask what happened next."

"I told Fenton that I would deal with him later, and I hit the bouncer with a handy Bud bottle. Things began to deteriorate rapidly from that point. The bouncer was bleeding from a nasty scalp wound and that ass Fenton was trying to help the bastard. Willis looked like a deer in the headlights and the owner reached behind the bar to grab what I guessed would be a baseball bat. Wrong, Charley, it was a Remington 870 Pump .12 gauge."

"This would constitute a definite escalation in weaponry. What was your next move?"

"I considered the situation for about a millisecond and determined that discretion was the better part of valor and hauled ass out the front door before anyone could react. I made the shoulder of Highway 82 before the first shot was fired. I felt the sting of a load of bird shot, but I was far enough away that I don't think it did much damage."

"That probably explains the blood dripping down on your boot. I was curious about that."

"Oh, shit, maybe it did break the skin. Anyway, I was shifting into high gear running down the shoulder toward town when I decided to look over my shoulder to see where the dude with the shotgun might be and when I collided with one of those highway signs on the steel post. I took the sign down, but the impact caused me to veer to my left and go crashing into the woods along the river bank."

"I'm beginning to see a pattern develop here. How did this lead to Billy Bob and the hunting party?"

"After I reached the river, I decided to work my way along the bank until I had put some serious distance between me and that Remington. I slipped about a half mile upstream and decided that it was probably safe to try to go back to the road. I found a little dirt road leading in the right direction and made it a couple of hundred yards when I saw four guys in a pickup truck unloading a pack of beagles."

"My guess is you thought you saw salvation and assistance." Benny said.

"Yeah, I was about to walk up and ask for a ride back to camp when I noticed that one of them had blood all over his shirt and a big towel wrapped around his head. He and I recognized each other about the same time. I ran, they chased, and the rest you guys saw play out."

"If we don't play this just right, this is going to crack the officers on your court martial completely up. They may agree to life at hard labor rather than a firing squad." I said.

"Come on guys, no shit, what am I gonna do?"

"Keep your mouth shut and leave it to me and Benny. It won't be pretty, but you will probably slide on the serious stuff. Millstone may kill you, but we gotta take that risk"

"My ass is in your hands."

"Now there's a scary thought."

It was almost 11:00 and the guard would soon be changing. The first thing we had to do was get George back to the company area undetected. This would require some world -lass begging. We told George to wash the blood off as best he could before Benny took him back up to the pickup point on the dirt road and hid him in the brush. We returned to our stations and awaited our relief.

Soon the weapons carrier came bumping and rattling down the road to post 24. My replacement came picking his way to the river bank where I challenged him and he gave the proper reply. He formally relived me of my post and I headed back to the waiting vehicle. When I got there, I asked the Corporal of the guard if I could bend his ear for a quick moment. This guy was from the Meadville unit and I didn't know him from Adam's off ox, but I had to try."

"My friend, who we will pick up at Post 23, and I have a little personal problem and we need your help. I promise it won't cost you anything and you can't get into trouble," I began.

The corporal looked at me with a skeptical air and said,

"What kind of personal problem?"

"One of the guys in our company got a little drunk in town and got his ass whipped pretty bad. He's cut up a little and needs to sneak back into the company area without a lot of fanfare."

"How in the hell did he get out here in the middle of nowhere?"

"He swam the river just ahead of a bunch a loggers and airmen who wanted to finish the job they had started on him."

"He let a bunch of blue pukes whip his ass?"

"Naw, I think it was mostly the loggers."

"What's your plan?"

"Just let him ride shotgun as if he were your buddy and we can drop him off before we get to the Officer of the Day; we'll take it from there."

"Oh, what the hell, the 155th has to stick together at times like this. Bring him on up here."

I whistled, and George came out of the brush and climbed into the passenger's seat next to the driver. We jarred our way back toward the camp, picking up guards at every post. When we got near the camp, the guy stopped the truck and George climbed out.

"Hide in those trees over there until we come and get you. It may be fifteen to twenty minutes, but don't leave that cover until we call you. Got it?"

"Yeah, I got it. Hurry if you can, my back is beginning to really hurt."

"We'll be back as soon as we can."

We rode back to the Officer of the Day's setup where we were duly dismissed from guard duty. We thanked the guy from Meadville and promised to buy him a beer at the Service Club when we got to McClellan. We hurried back to the company area and quickly hunted down Jesse.

"You gotta be shitting me," Jesse said when we related the bare facts of the problem. "Okay, here's where we start. I'm going to take this to Maggio, we'll need his blessing to move forward. My guess is that he will be willing to bump the problem up to Lt. Young, the acting company C.O. Once it is in the hands of an officer there are two ways it could go."

"Two ways, huh?" I replied.

"Yeah, he can decide to do this by the book and place George under arrest pending further investigation and possible disciplinary action, or he can decide to handle it as if it is a company-level matter.

"Oh, shit, we are all gonna be f**ked." Benny moaned.

"Not necessarily," Jesse said. "Millstone doesn't like anyone screwing with his troops, especially some civilians. I'm willing to bet this gets handled tonight without outside interference. Let me go see Maggio and start the ball rolling, You guys go back to get George and all of you stay in the company area. I suspect that Millstone will want to see all three of you. I'm going to get the medics to come over and look at George's wounds. They can do this as a routine injury until Millstone makes his determination."

"Thanks, man, we'll be waiting to hear what you want us to do."

Benny and I quickly gathered up George and went back to the company area. As soon as we got George settled in, the medics showed up and began working on his injuries. He had one #6 pellet under his scalp several in his back and three in his ass. None had penetrated too deeply so the medics removed the shot and cleaned and bandaged the small holes left in George. They gave him a mild pain killer and sent him to his sack. Benny and I waited to hear from Jesse.

It wasn't twenty minutes until Jesse came and called us to come to the Company HQ. It seemed that Captain Millstone wanted to hear a firsthand account of the evening's events. With some apprehension we followed Jesse.

We reported to Millstone. He put us at ease and said,

"Tell me exactly what took place tonight. Don't leave anything out."

We related the night's events beginning with the far-off shots and the subsequent dog run. We left nothing out.

"How is Bines, has he seen the medics?"

"Yes, sir, they picked the bird shot out and treated the wounds. They gave him some pain killer and sent him to his tent. They said he should be able return to full duty in the morning."

"Do you know the name of the joint that this started in?"

"George said it was called the Hi Hat. According to him it is across the Tombigbee on the way to Starkville."

"Thank you. You men are dismissed and can return to the company area. I'd get some sleep, we have busy day tomorrow."

We snapped to attention and saluted smartly. Millstone returned the salute and turned to Maggio and we heard him say,

"Pauli, get about four of your guys into civvies and meet me back here in ten minutes. Carr, get changed, you are going to be our stalking horse."

We decided that the less we knew about what was coming next, the better off we would be. We went to bed and were soon asleep under our little tent.

Whistles blew and NCO's screamed, "Get outta your racks, drop your cocks and grab your socks. The 155th is about to move out."

This was our version of reveille. No bugles, just Italians kicking and screaming. It was very effective and we were soon standing the first formation of the day.

The platoon sergeants reported, "All present or accounted for," to the First Sergeant, and Maggio made his report to Lt. Young. I noticed two things right off the bat. Captain Millstone was standing with his hands on his hips at the edge of the formation, and George Bines was nowhere to be seen.

Lt. Young gave us the daily scoop and when he finished he said,

"Captain Millstone would like to address the company at this time." He did an about face and yelled,

"Company E reporting as ordered, Sir!"

Millstone put the company at ease and began, "Late last night, persons unknown, dressed in civilian clothes, attacked the owner and three of the employees of the Hi Hat Club in Columbus. There was serious injury to all four of the victims and all are being treated at the Columbus Hospital."

As convoy Commander, I am responsible for the welfare and safety of every man in this Regiment. In that capacity, in conjunction with the local authorities, I have conducted a thorough investigation of this incident and have officially reported to the Columbus police department that no member of the Mississippi National Guard was in anyway associated with this regrettable attack. Our joint investigation, did however, determine that the perpetrators of this outrage were very large men of Italian descent. It is now suspected that they were members of the New Orleans Mafia attempting to collect gambling debts. The investigation is now in the hands of State and local law enforcement agencies."

"I have detached a two man team to precede the convoy to Fort McClellan to prepare our company area. This team is composed of

138

Sgt. Jesse Carr and PFC George Bines; they pulled out late last night and will meet up with us later today. That is all. Lt. Young you may dismiss the Company."

We ate our breakfast, broke camp, policed our area, got on the trucks and headed for Fort McClellan, secure in the knowledge that justice had been done.

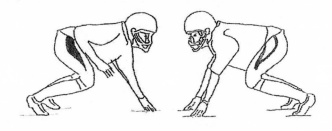

An Evening With Marvin

It was the football season of 1955 and I was starting at defensive guard on the Cumberland Bulldogs. I was a sophomore this year and had lettered the year before, but this was my first year to be a starter. Five of my 10th grade teammates and I had been playing on the high school team since the eighth grade, and this year we were playing in every game.

When we first came out in the eighth grade, Cumberland had just come off a Delta Valley Conference Championship and almost everyone had graduated. The coaches were desperate for players and we had jumped at the chance. Not only had we paid our dues over the past three years, but we had matured physically. I was 5'9" and weighed 165 in the eighth grade. I started this year at 6'2" and 228. We were enjoying the first winning season in Cumberland since that Championship year.

The Delta Valley Conference had three senior-laden, outstanding teams in 1955 and we had already played one of them. Yazoo City was loaded with talent and ran the new T formation that had been introduced by Coach Bobby Dobb of Georgia Tech. They had beaten us badly early in the season. Winona had one of the best athletes to grace the Mississippi high school scene in years, a quarterback named Billy Stacy. He was a senior and was being recruited by half of the Southeastern Conference. We would be playing them in our next to last game. Tonight we would be going up against Indian Springs on the road. They were 6-0 and we were 5-1. Everyone was expecting a good close game and we were thinking upset.

The seventh period bell rang and most of the students hung around the campus planning to go to the girls' gym for the pre-game pep rally starting at 5:00. I pitched my books in my locker, grabbed my letter jacket and set out to the team meeting in the football locker room. I met up with Benny on my way to the boys' gym and he fell into step beside me.

"Got your game face on?" he asked.

"You know I don't believe in that crap. I have never understood why banging my head on a locker would make me a better football player."

"Your problem is that you have a deep-seated dislike for authority."

"Well, there's that too, but I don't need to conjure up additional hostility, I'm plenty damn hostile; as it is."

"You know what they say about good football players; they should be 'mobile, agile and hostile."

"Yeah, and the greatest of these is 'hostile."

We entered the gym and joined in the general hubbub of players starting to get the pre-game jitters. Everybody gets a little edgy just before a game; we called it getting "butterflies in your stomach." Some guys got so worked up that they would vomit and nearly have a nervous breakdown before the first licks were passed. A whistle blast quieted down the mob scene and Coach Wiley signaled for everyone to take a knee and listen up.

"By this time in the season y'all should know the drill, but since some of you have the attention span of a retarded yard chicken we are going over it one more time. I am going to cover the whole game plan before we breakdown into offense and defense. There are a couple of the brighter guys who will be going both ways and y'all will have to decide which side of the ball you need to work on most; it'll be up to you. I'm turning the meeting over to Coach Biles who will lay out the game plan."

Coach Lacey Biles was our assistant head coach and offensive coordinator. He plunged right into the game plan.

"Both teams will be running the single wing, but Indian Springs does it with a slight twist. They will come out with an over-shifted line on every play. They will have two guards between the center and tackle, and this could be strong side right or strong side left. Coach Kemp will cover how we intend to defend against this when we break up into offense and defense."

Coach John Kemp nodded his agreement and Biles continued.

"Defensively they will be in a standard six-man front and they will over-shift to our strong side as we go from right to left with our blocking back and wing back. They are particularly strong on defense and probably have the best linebackers and defensive halfbacks in the conference. Nobody's been able to run on them this year, and they are tough defending against the pass. We've put in a couple of variations on offense to confuse them and maybe give us an advantage."

Coach Wiley took over and said, "Okay, let's break up into offense and defense. The pep rally starts at 5:00 and I sure don't want you lads to miss your inspiration."

The defense moved to the rear of the gym and gathered around Coach Kemp and Coach Slade, the defensive line coach. Coach Kemp walked up to the chalk boards and started laying out our defensive game plan. Seeing that we had been practicing this all week, it wasn't much of a surprise, but we knew better than to act bored. Coach Kemp went through the overall plan and quickly turned the linemen over to Coach Slade.

"Well, girls, here we are again, playing a team with a hell of a lot better players than we have. Since y'all may be the least talented players in the DVC, it is good that you have such a superior coaching staff. It is my job to make chicken salad out of chicken shit. It's a large task, but one that I am willing to accept."

"When I look down the Indian Springs offensive line I see three, maybe four seniors who will be playing on Saturday next year, most probably in the SEC. They have two ends that are top notch. Larry Smith, their strong side end, he'll line up on the over-shifted strong side on every play. He maybe the best blocking end in the conference; he weighs in at 220 and is 6'3"."

"Their other end is a speedster with good hands. His name is Kent Loveland and he is a sprinter in track and their favorite receiver. We'll have to double cover him or he will eat our lunch. Their weak side linemen are just ordinary; in fact, if we have an advantage at all it will be here. They seldom run to the weak side and when they do they pull the beef from the strong side to lead the play."

"Their strong side is something else. The center is a senior named Wayne Browner and he is huge. They carry him on the program at 255 and 6'5", but he probably he's more like 285 and 6'6'. That's the bad news; the good news is that he can hardly run out of his shadow; I'll have to admit that he cast a pretty big shadow. He is virtually immoveable, but he is also immobile and won't be a factor outside of his three or four-yard area. We'll just have to run around him. Larch, you and Tong are going to be playing nose- up on Browner all evening. Think you can handle him?"

What was I going to say, "No coach, probably not, he'll just beat us by himself"? I had been at this football business far too long to fall into that trap. In spite of being outweighed by thirty to fifty pounds and being half a foot shorter I quickly snapped,

"John and I got him covered-coach; he'll be dragging his fat ass around looking for an escape route when we finish with him. He's nothing but a tub of lard."

"Now that's the attitude I like. Larch is not intimidated by Browner and will take care of that problem."

Right, I thought, Browner is nothing but a tub of slow moving lard. Of course he can probably outrun our backs and can bench press a John Deere. He shouldn't be a problem.

Coach Slade moved on to the two strong side guards. The outside guard was named Marvin Terrell and not a lot was known about him. He was about 6 feet and close to 200 pounds. This was his first year to start and he played in the shadow of their super star, "Buck" McKinney. McKinney had been All-DVC for the past two years. He was 6'1" and 230 and they said he could run with the backs. He was the most intensely recruited high school lineman in Mississippi and it was assumed that he could not be handled by any one man.

When Coach Slade had finished his press conference on the many skills of Buck McKinney, he turned again to me and said.

"Larch, you may be able to hold your own against Browner, but we are going to have to get you some help with McKinney. I want you to shift to the outside and play nose-up on the Terrell kid. John Tong will move over on Browner's nose and the two of you will have to neutralize McKinney. I doubt that this Terrell guy will cause you much of a problem and you can concentrate on helping Tong with Browner and McKinney. Capiche?"

"I got it Coach; John and I'll take care of them."

The meeting moved on to how we planned to stop their passing game which only involved us linemen in the hope that we could put a little pressure on their tailback and not give him all day to throw. The single wing was primarily a running formation and pass plays generally took a while to develop and were usually nothing more than an attempt to keep our defensive backs honest. If we could get at the passer, all the better, but in the meantime somebody needed to knock down a couple of pulling guards, a blocking back and a fullback. Penetration was the key to taming the single wing.

The team meeting finally broke up about a quarter to five and we were free to attend the pep rally that would soon be starting. Benny and I walked over to the Girls' gym, took off our shoes and joined the rest of the team gathering at center court. You might ask why we removed our shoes? There was a very good answer to that question. We did it to save our ass.

The girls' gym was owned and operated by Coach Margaret "Peggy" Woods, the Cumberland girls' basketball coach. Coach Woods had won a stack of DVC championships and multiple State titles and treated her domain with the same attitude Attila displayed toward Hunsville. To say she was protective really didn't do her justice. Nobody walked on Peggy Woods' shiny gym floor in street shoes, or at least you only did it once; I mean nobody, not even W.J. Parks, the Superintendent of Schools, would do it twice.

The band began to play the Cumberland fight song and the bleachers were full of singing and cheering students. It was amazing what winning a couple of games could do for school spirit. During our three-year-run of losing we may have had a couple of hundred students and parents at a pep rally. Today the gym was totally packed with people standing along the edges of the court in their socks. Many were alums and knew the wrath of Peggy Woods.

The band played, the cheerleaders cheered and the coaches and captains made totally inane speeches about our loyalty and devotion to old Cumberland High. The rally broke up with the band playing the Cumberland High alma mater and it was clear that not ten people knew the score, let alone the lyrics.

The students and parents left to go home and get ready to drive to Indian Springs for the 8:00 kickoff. The band and cheerleaders headed to their buses and the team meandered back to the locker room.

John Tong caught me at my locker and sat down on the bench. John was one of the third generation Chinese Americans whose ancestors had come to the Delta with the railroad in the 1880's. John's grandfather had done manual labor on the railroad, his father owned a small grocery store in the Negro section of town, and John would go to Mississippi State and become a CPA. Three generations to the American Dream. He looked at me and said,

"What do you think about the game plan?"

"Hell, John, you know that all the planning goes out the window when the whistle blows. Can you and I handle Browner and McKinney? Probably not, a lot depends on just how good this Terrell kid is. If I can handle him and give you some help with the other two, we might just make it work."

"Well, you certainly sounded confident in the meeting."

"I hope you didn't buy that load of crap, it was just 'coach talk'."

"Coach talk, what in the hell is that?"

"John, when an intellectual giant like Coach Slade asks you a question, it is purely rhetorical. He knows the response he wants and if you don't feed it to him, he'll eat your ass out. I'd rather get chewed out if we can't get the job done rather than listen to it beforehand. Who knows? Terrell might be a complete chicken shit and we can manhandle the other two."

"So, you think we can maybe handle it?"

"I don't really know, let's just fake it "till we make it."

"Thanks," John said, as he walked away, "I can't say that I feel any better, but I guess we'll know soon enough."

If this were a home game, we'd be in the school cafeteria eating our pre-game carbo stuff. But since this was going to be played in Indian Springs, we would get our uniforms on, sans shoulder pads, and get on the team bus. Sack meals would be passed out and we would eat them on the way.

I was getting my ankles taped by one of the managers when I watched an unfolding drama just across the room. Buddy Clements was sitting in front of his locker looking completely baffled. Buddy played defensive end, the single wing suicide position. He feared no man or beast; he was a little shaky around girls, but that was another story.

Tonight he was dealing with something that completely bum-fuzzled him; math. He was holding his white game jersey, trying to decide how to put it on. Finally he turned to the manager taping my feet and said,

"Carter, how in the hell do I get this damn jersey on?"

"Gee, Buddy, I think I would start by sticking my head and arms through those holes."

"Don't give me any shit, I got that part, I just need to know which side goes in front."

"Okay," Carter sighed, "Put the small number in front and the big number in back."

"I already told you not to give me any shit. Both of the numbers are the same, 86."

Carpenter looked at Buddy with complete disdain and said,

"Goddamn, Clements, are you retarded?"

Since Carter and I had been friends since grammar school, I thought this might be a good place to step in and help. If I could defuse the situation it might just save Carter's ass.

"Hell, Buddy, I have the same problem myself. Here's a little trick I learned. Look in the neck hole and find the tag. Just remember the tag goes in back. Carter is a bit out of his element seeing that he has never put on a football jersey."

"Yeah, thanks, the little turd could have told me that."

"He'll know next time." I said and signaled Carter to keep his mouth shut.

Having solved his jersey problem, Buddy left to go to the bus. I turned to Carter, who was putting the finishing touches on my tape job and said,

"Tommy, one day you are going to let your alligator mouth overload your hummingbird ass and I'm not going to be there to save you. Buddy Clements may well be a little retarded, hell, he may be as dumb as a bucket of pig spit, but that doesn't mean that you have to point it out."

"You don't think I could take Clements?"

"Carter, I don't think you could take his little sister."

"I might like to try his little sister on for size; maybe we could set up a wrestling match."

"I just hope you remain alive until football season is over, you tape a mean ankle."

"Fuck you, Larch, and the horse you rode in on."

"You're welcome, you little twit."

I grabbed my shoulder pads and helmet and boarded the bus for Indian Springs. I slipped into the seat Benny was saving for me and flopped down holding my gear.

"Let me stick that stuff under our seat," Benny said, "you look like a thunder storm. What's up?"

"I had to pull Carter's foot out of his mouth again. He was giving Clements a ration of shit and was walking mighty close to the line."

"You ever think about just letting him try to handle stuff by himself?"

"Yeah, all the time, but I don't want to see him killed. Besides, he kinda depends on me."

"It's nice to be needed, isn't it?"

"It has its moments. I guess you and I need to decide how we're going to play this genius defense that Slade has come up with."

Benny would be playing inside linebacker just behind Tong and me and would be primarily responsible for stuffing up the running game. We always worked out a system that allowed Benny to cover an open hole if either John or I stunted.

"How y'all gonna play it tonight?" Benny asked.

"Won't really know till we get going, but if I can handle Terrell, then you and John can pretty much play it straight with the other two."

"Think you can handle him?"

"I don't see why not; I've never met a guy I couldn't handle one-on-one."

"Then we'll be in good shape. They won't be able to run in the middle.'

The managers came down the bus aisle passing out sack lunches. I took mine and looked inside. A tuna fish sandwich and a bag of chips looked back at me.

"Fucking tuna fish before a football game, gimme a break."

"Well, it's your fault, aren't you some kinda Catholic? It is Friday, you know."

"Benny, you know damn well I'm not a mackerel snapper, I'm an Episcopalian."

"Pretty much the same difference, isn't it?"

I knew Benny well enough to know when he was screwing with me and decided not to return the ball.

"What did you get? I might be willing to trade."

"I got ham and there is no possibility of a trade."

"Hey," I shouted, "anybody want to trade for my tuna sandwich?"

I was shouted down with about forty sarcastic comments about my sandwich and I decided to eat the damn thing and hope I didn't see it coming up later. The bus made the 33- mile trip to Indian Springs while we were eating our sandwiches and we soon pulled into the brightly lit home of the Indian Springs Indians.

Since most of the little high schools in the DVC did not have visitors' locker rooms, we used our bus as our home away from home. We finished dressing, putting on our pads and game jerseys, then filed off the bus and jogged to the far end zone to have our pre-game obligatory pep talk. This frustrated some of the more gung-ho guys since there were no lockers to bang their heads on. The goal post would have to do.

From our vantage point in the end zone we had a perfect view of an October harvest moon just peeking its nose over the horizon. The evening promised to be perfect for a football game, pleasantly cool with clear skies and a light breeze. The stands began to fill and the Indian Springs band was on the field with a pre- game show. Cumberland and Indian Springs were about the same size and since it was only 33 miles separating them we had almost as many fans as they did. There just wasn't a hell of a lot to do on Friday night.

When the band completed its show, the Indian Springs Indians came racing onto the field, led by their cheerleaders and pep squad. The band played their fight song and the home crowd cheered. I noticed Benny paying close attention to the cheerleaders and pep squad.

"Well, Bowman, I'm glad you've got your mind narrowly focused on the upcoming game."

"Yeah, I've been paying close attention to their personnel; seems to be a bumper crop this year."

"Prenatal care and good nutrition has done wonders for teenage girls."

Coach Wiley's whistle blew and we all gathered around him. He briefly went over the game plan and quickly began his little pre-game inspirational. Rig Wiley didn't hold with oratorical rhetoric and he was no great public speaker. He had seen far too much war to have any illusions about what motivated men.

He believed in loyalty and responsibility- first to the guy next to you, never let him down. Secondly, to the team who depended on you to tote your assigned load. Past that, screw 'em all and let God sort 'em out.

He pointed out that football required only two things of you. First to defeat and destroy the guy in front of you, take him completely out of the mix. Secondly, to be there at the end, stronger, faster and more determined than your opponent. He and the coaches would provide the conditioning that would allow you to do this; the will was up to you.

Finally he pointed out that a high school football game lasted only 48 minutes. If all things were equal and offense and defense played the same amount of time this was only 24 minutes. If it took 20 seconds to call a play, get lined up and go through the snap cadence, and the play itself took a max of ten seconds to be completed, then you only played football for about 8 minutes a game. If there was anyone who didn't feel that he could go full speed for 8 minutes, raise his hand and get the hell out of here.

We jumped to our feet and charged on to our end of the field to go through our pre-game warm-up drill. I'll have to admit that every time I heard Coach Wiley give that little talk it made me want to deliver my end of the bargain. Tonight I knew that John Tong and I had the task of neutralizing two of the best high school lineman in the State of Mississippi. I had every intention of screwing their evening completely up. Browner and McKinney didn't have any idea what was coming.

The two teams lined up for the opening kickoff. Indian Springs had won the coin toss and had chosen to kick to us and go on defense. I am forced to admit that I was never on a kickoff team, neither kicking nor receiving. I was just too damn slow. I was fairly quick within a three yard area, but way too slow to operate in the open field. I watched as the kick sailed down to our fifteen yard line and Mickey brought it back to the twenty-two.

We ran three running plays that netted a total of four yards and T.C. punted it away. Indian Springs had the ball first and ten at their own thirty-three yard line. They came out in their over shifted single wing and I moved head-up on Marvin Terrell, the outside guard. The following eight minutes, if that is indeed how long you actually play football, provided me with a life changing experience. It is amazing that a mere eight minutes can seem like several days.

The Indian Springs tailback called the snap cadence and Browner snapped the ball. I was prepared to receive McKinney's charge on my left and play off Terrell to my right. McKinney disappeared and I felt myself being carried completely out of the play and watched helplessly as the Indian Springs fullback sailed through the hole I was supposed to be defending for an eight-yard gain.

I had no idea what had happened. Apparently McKinney had pulled behind Terrell and blocked down on our tackle and somehow I had been swept out of the way. I had not felt any impact from Terrell, it was as if he simply ushered me away. Talk about confused, I was totally baffled.

On the next play McKinney hit me high and Terrell hit me low and once again I saw the fullback zoom by untouched. First-and-ten from the Indian Springs forty-eight. On the next play the tailback hit Loveland with a fifty-yard touchdown pass and our defense was off the field. I jogged to the sidelines and sat down beside John tong.

"Well, that really went well." he said.

"I have no idea exactly what happened. One minute I was in position and the next I was nowhere near the play."

"Do you think maybe you got blocked?"

"Well, I got that part, I just don't know how."

"The word 'completely' comes to mind."

"Well, I can guarantee you that won't happen again."

But it did, not only on the next series, but all night long. I totally ignored McKinney and Browner and let Tong deal with them. Marvin Terrell became the sole focus of my attention. I tried every trick and technique that I knew to defeat his block. Nothing worked. You can't hit what you can't catch.

I have tried over the years to describe what playing head-up on Terrell was like and it defies every football cliché that I know. This was not the only Friday night I got handled by an offensive lineman. The difference was that in the other cases I could explain exactly how it happened. They were either bigger, quicker or stronger and in some cases all three. They would hit you like a run-away Mack truck and bulldoze you out of the play.

Terrell was different. True, he was quicker and stronger and I know that played a part, but the only way to describe him is to say that he was 'elegant'. He exploded in your face like a hand grenade and simply placed you where he wanted you to be. His upper body strength was impressive, but his ability to drive his legs and scoop you up was even more impressive. It was as if I was playing against a ghost or a whiff of smoke. I cannot remember but a couple of plays that I had any part in tackling someone, and then only because I was McKinney's responsibility, not Terrell's.

Usually, when you are getting your butt handed to you the game seems interminably long. This one flew by. By the middle of the fourth quarter Terrell was giving me hands-on coaching advice. He suggested that I try to keep my initial charge lower and not let him into my body mass. He felt that I needed to work on my upper body strength and try to keep my legs churning after contact. I listened to what he said, but to tell you the truth, none of his advice made much difference. He just had his way with me all night.

When the game ended we had actually played one of our best games all year. They beat us 14-7, which surprised everyone including Coach Wiley. When the whistle ending the game blew, I walked across the field, found Terrell and said,

"Believe it or not, I enjoyed playing against you. You're far and away the best football lineman I have ever been up against. Tonight was a real learning experience."

Terrell looked at me and said,

"Thanks, I appreciate the compliment. Keep on learning. You can be a good player yourself."

We shook hands and I said,

"Thanks for the coaching clinic; I learned just how much I don't know. Good luck for the rest of the season, hope you guys win it all."

I walked back to our end zone and met my Dad on the way.

"Tommy," he said, "I'm surprised your uniform shows any dirt or grass stains."

"I take it you have some fatherly advice you're about to share."

"No advice, just an observation. The next time you want to go to a football game as a spectator, buy a ticket and sit in the stands. That little guy beat your ass all over this field."

"That he did," I admitted, "he was something else. We can go over my mistakes later; I got to get on the bus now."

"I'll be surprised if they let you on the bus, they oughta make you walk back to Cumberland."

"Thanks again, Dad, I'll see you at home."

He walked off shaking his head. I took off my shoulder pads and put my jersey back on and got on the bus. I found my seat next to Benny and sat down.

"Good game," he said.

"Yeah," I replied, "I'll probably be on the "B" team next week after they review the game film."

"Why do you say that?"

"I just got my ass waxed; that's the worst game I ever played."

"I played right behind you and I didn't think you looked all that bad."

"That's because Marvin Terrell led me around like I had a ring in my damn nose."

"Well, you and Tong kept Browner and McKinney from being much of a factor."

"John gets all of the credit for that. All I did was provide Terrell with an evening of mild amusement. Like I told my Dad, tonight was a complete learning experience."

"Really, what did you learn?"

"If Marvin Terrell represents a typical college prospect, then I better let go of the notion of ever playing on the next level."

Indian Springs went on to win 1955 Delta Valley Conference Championship. Mississippi State beat out a dozen other schools and signed Buck McKinney. He never made a difference at State. Ole Miss was the only school willing to take a chance on Marvin Terrell.

He started at guard for three years and was All-SEC and a consensus All-American his senior year. He played four years for the Dallas Texans in the old American Football League. Marvin Terrell proved to be the real deal.

A Liberal Education

It was Labor Day 1957 and sunrise was 6:12 am. I knew this, because I had already been up for over an hour. Benny and I planned to pull out of Cumberland by 9:00 at the latest. It was 155 miles to Starkville, all on busy two lane roads. I figured it would take us about three and a half hours to get there. My grandparents had given me a used 1950 Ford Business Coup for High School Graduation and it could best be described as basic transportation. There were no frills, not even a back seat. No heater and no radio. We're talking basic here. I was damn glad to have it.

I loaded my gear into the trunk and was in the process of eating breakfast before I picked Benny up to head out. This was clearly a special occasion; the whole family was seated around the kitchen table. I was pretty sure this was the first time this had ever happened. Not only were we eating breakfast together, my mother was actually cooking bacon and eggs. I looked at my little brother, George, and said, "Don't let this scare you, little guy, I'm sure you'll be back on the oatmeal plan starting tomorrow."

"Can I have your coin collection? You won't need it at Mississippi State."

"I don't want you anywhere near my room or my stuff while I'm gone. I'll be coming home at Thanksgiving and I swear if you've touched a single thing, you're gonna suffer a slow and painful death."

"Don't talk to your brother like that, you'll scare him," cautioned my mother.

"That's exactly the point. He better be scared if he knows what's good for him."

"Let's change the subject," my mother said, "I want things to be nice on your last morning at home."

"Good Lord, Kathleen, the boy's only going to college, not Katmandu, " my father said while continuing to read the Memphis Commercial Appeal, "It's enough that you organized this breakfast;

the kid will soon be 18 and this may be the first time you ever fixed him bacon and eggs."

"Yeah, all I ever get is soggy oatmeal." George whined

I looked at my watch and it was nearly 8:30. I needed to go pick up Benny. I polished off the rest of my breakfast and chugged down my glass of orange juice.

"Thanks Mom, the breakfast was really good. The car's all loaded and I need to hit the trail. See you guys at Thanksgiving." I edged toward the kitchen door.

"Be sure and write us every week and let us know how you're doing with your studies. And be sure to be careful."

Ah, there it was, the final maternal admonition had been said. I could leave at last.

"Bye, Dad, hope you can come to some football games. I still plan to walk on and try to make the team."

"Good Luck," he said. "I'll probably try to come to the Tennessee and Alabama games. We'll see."

"If I can't have the coin collection, how 'bout the stamps?" George chirped.

"Do it and you're a dead squirt, squirt."

And so my life in higher education began.

I drove the three blocks to Benny's house and helped him throw his gear in the space that would have normally housed a back seat. It didn't take a minute, neither of us had much by way of belongings. Benny's mom and dad went through the mandatory parental goodbye shtick, and all but hustled us out of the driveway. Mr. Bowman needed to make his tee time at the Country Club and Mrs. Bowman wanted to finish getting ready for her bridge club's weekly meeting.

"Well, they seem to be holding up well under the grief of losing you to the big, bad world." I said.

"Yeah', bye Benny, don't let the doorknob catch you in the ass. Mom will have one of her decorator buddies picking out paint and fabric for her new guest room before the weeks out. All my stuff will probably wind up at Goodwill."

"You win some, you lose some and some get rained out."

"Goddamn, you need to major in philosophy when we get to State. Deep thoughts like that are really profound."

"Profound this," I said, shooting him the bird.

Early fall in the Mississippi Delta was still hot in the middle of the day, but the mornings and evenings had begun to cool off. In other places it would be Indian summer, in the Delta it was dove season. The Delta's annual cycle consisted of planting cotton and turkey hunting in the spring, sweltering, fishing and chopping cotton in the summer, doves, football and picking cotton in the fall and quail, ducks, deer and geese bracketing Christmas and New Years in the winter. It was great place to grow up and we were leaving it, probably for good.

The morning air was still cool as we drove east on Highway 8 passing Dockery Plantation and turning North at Abbeville to finally intersect U.S. 82 at Moorhead. Moorhead was famous as the site at which the Yellow crossed the Dog. I knew this because I'd read it on one of those big green signs decorated with Magnolias erected by the Mississippi Department of Archives. I supposed that there was some historical significance to this, but in our circle Moorhead was better known as the home of Sunflower Junior College, a football farm club for Ole Miss and State. We affectionately referred to it as Sunset Tech.

All we had to do was stay on U.S. 82 for another 112 miles and we would be there. The only time either one of us had been to Mississippi State was for football games or the trip our Boy Scout troop took to the Raspert Flight Center to fly in gliders. The Scouts had camped out at the airport, so we knew less than nothing about

State or Starkville. That's why we were going today, a week before classes started. We wanted to go to orientation which started at noon. We weren't all that concerned about the details, there would be 1500 other freshman starting at the same time we did. How hard could it be?

The balance of the trip passed pleasantly with Benny and me talking about hunting, fishing, football and girls. Higher education never came up. We were about 10 miles out of Starkville when I said, "Benny, did you bring that letter about orientation with the directions of how to do it?"

"Mom may have stuck it in with the other crap they've been sending us, let me look."

He scrounged around in a big manila envelope and finally came up with three mimeographed pages titled MISSISSIPPI STATE COLLEGE, FRESHMAN ORIENTATION 1957.

"Here it is, what'cha want to know?"

"What's our first move?"

"I suspect we need to find a place to park as close to Lee Hall as we can. That's where the process starts."

"Lee Hall it is."

The traffic started to pick up on the outskirts of Starkville and by the time we were on College Drive and following the signs to Mississippi State it was bumper to bumper. College Drive wound under a canopy of large oak trees and was lined by houses and apartment buildings. Finally the traffic drew us through the two brick pillars that marked the entrance to the State campus and the scenery changed drastically.

There were wide swaths of manicured lawns scattered with large old oak trees. An active railroad line paralleled College Drive and had been integrated into the landscape plan. Across the railroad embankment stood a stately row of large two story columned homes. It made for an impressive entrance and Benny and I were gawking like the rubes we were.

The long line of cars continued to creep forward as we approached an intersection with five streets converging to one central point. We would later call this "malfunction junction" like everybody else that had to deal with driving through it. On a football Saturday, it was impassable. Scott Field, the large concrete football stadium, loomed on our left, marking the center of the campus. There were dorms and buildings lining both sides of the street, and soon we were opposite an enormous four-story brick building looming like a gothic prison. This was Old Main dormitory and our soon-to-be home-away-from-home.

As we passed Old Main we came to a traffic cop directing all of the traffic to a street that ran down the side of another three story building. We had found Lee Hall. We were directed to park in a very large and well-kept green space which we would later learn was the Drill Field. Today was the only day cars were allowed on the drill field long enough to get your orientation information and unload your gear in your room in Old Main. After this afternoon, parking would become the major problem in my life. There were very few parking spaces anywhere near Old Main. When it was built in 1878 the cadets at Mississippi A&M were not even allowed to keep a horse; they were expected to walk. The intervening 79 years had preserved that expectation.

I parked as close to Old Main as I could, and Benny and I walked across the drill field to Lee Hall. We quickly found the first of what would prove to be a bunch of long lines of waiting Freshman. We entered the end of a line that led to a large sign with a huge number 1 and the instructions, "START HERE".

"Why don't we start here," I said.

"Probably a good plan" replied Benny.

Eventually, we reached a long table with signs doing the A-H, I-P thing and lined up in another shorter line under the appropriate initials. When I got to the table I was asked my name and handed a thick packet of forms and instructions. I took the forms and asked the student at the table,

"Where to next?"

"Why don't you try that big sign over there that says 2?" You may be too dumb to be here." The little shit replied.

"Why don't you bite my ass?" I said with one of my best glares.

"Whatever," he muttered and turned to the next guy in line.

I joined Benny in line 2 and he offered an observation:

"I haven't seen many coeds in this process; in fact, I haven't seen any."

"I imagine they have their own system working, sorta like the boys' and girls' gyms at home."

"Yeah, that's probably it. I'm sure we'll see' em later."

We made it up to the number 2 table and discovered that we were assigned Room 331 in D section of Old Main. We were handed a couple of keys that looked like they had been made about 1776 and sent off to the next line. Line 3 got your student ID photo made and a temporary ID card. Line 4 was for a parking sticker with your parking priority expressed as a 1-5. I was a five. I suspected that a 5 parking priority put you somewhere between Ackerman and Sturgis, but nowhere near Old Main. This proved to be the exact case.

Our parents had paid all of our fees when they sent in our applications: $98.00 for tuition, $96.00 for our room and $100 for a one-semester food ticket, good for three student plates a day in the cafeteria. All in all, a hell of a bargain. We picked up our meal tickets at the last station.

By the time we completed the orientation maze it was close to 4:00 and we stopped by the car to grab our duffle bag before heading to Old Main. The ancient dormitory had been constructed section by section over seventy-plus years. The final result was four connected wings surrounding a central quadrangle, each side four stories tall and close to a quarter of a mile in length. There were arched entrances to the building about every fifty yards on each of the four sides. Benny and I had no idea where to find section D. There were no signs or directions, so we just went in the first of the arched entrances we came to and started asking for directions. Unfortunately almost everyone we asked was looking for his own section and the result was a complete cluster fuck.

Eventually somebody who had found D section while looking for A Section told us that it was just opposite the entrance to the cafeteria. A land mark at last. We found the cafeteria and confirmed that this was indeed section D.

"Well, at least we'll be close to the chow hall," Benny said. "Wonder where 331 will be?"

"Just a stab in the dark, but it may be on the third floor; let's check it out."

There was a steady stream of guys coming and going on the dark narrow stairwell that led to the upper floors of D section. About half of them had their heads shaved and were wearing silly looking little maroon caps with a big white M on them. Boy, did they look stupid.

"You know, school spirit is one thing, but to shave your head and wear a Howdy Doody hat is taking it too far." Benny said as we climbed the stairs dodging guys carrying their stuff up and those that were returning to get another load.

"Cool it, Benny, these guys could be Jewish, you know."

"Couldn't be that, there aren't this many Jews in the whole damn state."

"Yeah, you won't see me wearing one of those, you can bet your ass on that."

The ceilings in Old Main averaged about sixteen feet in height and there was a crawl space for plumbing and wiring between each level, so the third floor was about twice the distance from the ground as you would expect. This made for a long climb. Finally we reached the third floor and began looking for 331. Some of the rooms had a number and some didn't, but by the process of elimination we were able to locate what we thought to be our room. This was confirmed by the fact that the key opened the door. Later we would realize that the key opening the door was not much of a clue, all the keys opened all the doors.

Benny pushed the door open and we surveyed our new home. It was a very short survey. A large twenty by twenty space with wooden floors, plaster walls and two floor- to-ceiling windows that looked out over the cafeteria across the way. A bare light bulb hung by a wire from a hole in the ceiling illuminating two iron bunk beds. That was it. I looked at Benny and he looked at me. He finally said,

"It's gonna take a little fixin' up, but it is much bigger than I expected."

"I hope it's big enough for us and that big guy sitting on your mattress." I said, pointing to the perhaps three-pound wharf rat glaring at us from across the room.

"Oh shit," Benny moaned, "I hate goddamn rats. Why don't you chase his ass outta here?"

"I don't know about chasing him out, he looks pretty comfortable to me. Maybe you could sleep on the floor until he decides to leave."

The huge rat wiggled his nose, gave us a parting glare and calmly exited through a crack in the corner of the room. His whole attitude indicated that he would be back whenever the urge came upon him.

"We probably oughta stop up that crack over there," Benny said.

"Let's wait and see. I don't want to piss him off." I replied.

"Yeah, don't want him pissed off, that's for sure."

Since neither of us had ever seen the inside of a dormitory room we were not offended by the absence of any plumbing, even a small wash basin. As far as we knew, the rooms at Princeton were just like this. The ten-man tents at Fort McClellan didn't have plumbing and we were pretty comfortable there. What you don't know is sometimes a big advantage.

There seemed to be nothing to do but throw our duffle bags on the beds and start hauling up the rest of our gear. As we were locking our door a guy with a shaved head and one of those silly hats walked up and stuck out his hand.

"Hi, I'm Roy Ruddy from Belzoni, Mickey Braswell and I have the room across the hall. You guys need any help with your stuff?"

"Hi Roy, I'm Tom Larch and this is Benny Bowman. We're from Cumberland. Thanks for offering, but I think we can manage."

"I just gotta ask you something. Why in the hell did you cut off all of your hair and where did you get that dumb little hat?" Benny said with a big smile.

"I figured it better to go on and get it cut than to wait for some upperclassmen to make a big deal out of cutting it for me. All freshman are gonna get their head shaved, it's up to you how hard you want to make the process. As for the Beanie, you have to have one. They are on sale at the bookstore for a buck each and you don't want to be caught in public without one."

"What would happen if I decided not to play that game?"

"They would take you down, cut your hair and whip your ass. It may take ten of them to do it, but that won't really be a problem, there are a couple of thousand hoping you'll resist. If I were you, I'd just go along with the tradition; your hair will grow out soon enough."

"Benny, that makes a lot of sense to me; let's just go with the flow on this one."

Benny had that look he always got when someone tried to make him do something; it was usually followed by left jab and a quick combination of punches. He looked at me and said,

"Why not, it's all part of being a freshman. No problem."

"One more piece of advice while I'm on a roll." Ruddy said,

"If you brought your high school football letter jacket, don't wear it until you remove the letter. It really pisses the jocks off, and they will shuck you out of it and kick your ass."

"Well, shit" I said, "that's the only jacket I brought besides my hunting gear."

"Suit yourself, but at least you were forewarned," grinned Ruby.

"C'mon, Mickey and I will help you with the next load."

It took the four of us only one more trip to bring up the rest of our stuff including the four guns we brought for hunting. Benny and I had every intention of learning the lay of the land and where to hunt. Hunting was a part of our lives that we never even questioned. Everybody in Mississippi owned a bunch of guns, and hunting was an important part of our culture.

We thanked Ruddy and Braswell for their help and promised to holler at them before we went to the cafeteria for supper. We found some cardboard boxes that had been left in the hall and used them as a temporary substitute for a chest of drawers. We unpacked our extra underwear, jeans, shirts and socks and unloaded our duffle bags. We left our army fatigues neatly folded and stacked them in the footlockers we had placed at the foot of our beds. We put a set of sheets on the beds and covered them with our two army blankets, making sure the corners were neat and square. They could have passed inspection. We stuck our guns between the cot and the mattress until we figured out a better plan.

It was close to 6:00 by the time we finished getting the room squared away, and we were hot and sweaty. Even with the large windows wide open, there was hardly a breath of moving air.

"Bubba, we're gonna have to get us a fan. This place is like an oven." Benny bitched.

"Yeah, I hope it cools off before we go to bed, I'm soaked through to my skivvies. Believe I'm gonna grab a quick shower."

"Good idea," said Benny as we stripped off our sweaty clothes, grabbed a towel and our dop kits before we headed down the hall to find the head and the showers. We passed an open door that led to a tiled latrine area. There were wash basins along one wall, urinals and commodes along the other. Like all of the locker rooms and latrines we had ever seen there were no toilet seats on the commodes. Nothing new here, Standard Operating Procedure. The shower room proved to be something all together different.

Benny was poised just outside of a totally dark room without lights or windows. He was peering in with a look of wonder spreading across his face. He looked at me and said,

"This must be the shower; I hear water splashing in there."

I looked into the damp black hole and could hear the distinct sound of running water.

"Yeah, this must be it. I think I'll go and get my flashlight outta my hunting gear before we just rush in here."

I fetched the light and turned it on. Sure enough this was our shower area. I could see beer cans and broken beer bottles scattered around the room, and there were two streams of tepid water falling from somewhere near the ceiling. We took our dop kits back to the latrine area and folded our towels over them. Naked, we took a bar of soap and the flash light and returned to the shower room. I held the light while Benny showered and he did the same for me. We were headed back to the latrine when he said,

"Add some shower shoes to the fan list."

"Shower shoes my ass, let's get some rubber boots."

"Well, you can bet your sweet butt that will be my last shower barefoot. Athletes foot will probably prove to be a minor problem; I'm worried about leprosy or the Hungarian crotch rot."

We dried off and fru'ed up in the latrine and headed back to our room. We were about half way there when this motherly looking lady backed out of her son's room to see how the curtains she was hanging looked. We were too stunned to stop and strolled between her and the object of her decorating. It was hard to say who was the most surprised, but at least we didn't go screaming into our room. She did.

The recipient of the curtains sauntered out in to the hall and said,

"Sorry 'bout that, I tried to tell her, but she just couldn't grasp the concept of a 'Men's Dormitory'." I'm Larry Stockton from Biloxi and that's my mom."

"We didn't mean to give her such a start, but we had no idea there were women in the building. Think you can get her out of our room?"

"Yeah, just wrap the towel around you and stand still, she'll come out for me."

His mother came out of our room and quickly ran into his. She looked completely traumatized. We decided that she would soon be leaving, curtains or no curtains. When we were safely in our room and the door closed Benny said,

"Larry seemed like a nice enough guy; he took us flashing his mom pretty well."

"Yeah he did. I couldn't help but think if we caused her so much shock, what would she do if she ever saw Willy Slade coming out of the shower?"

"It would probably change her life."

Willy Slade had been our line coach at Cumberland High, and he held the record in the clubhouse for dong size. If Mom had seen that thing she would have never noticed Benny and me. We dressed in fresh jeans, Cumberland practice jerseys and tennis shoes. We were ready for something to eat.

"Let's check and see if Ruddy and Braswell want to go with us," Benny said.

We walked across the hall and knocked on their door.

"Come on in, we're almost ready. I've got a suggestion for y'all. There's a head shaving station set up just outside the cafeteria door so why don't y'all get it done and Mickey and I will go over to the bookstore and buy a couple of beanies for you. Maybe it will save getting harassed later on."

"Sounds like a good plan to me," I said.

"Sounds totally stupid to me, but I guess I don't really have a choice," Benny conceded.

We walked down the stairs to the cafeteria entrance and sure enough there was a bunch of upperclassmen laughing and shaving freshman heads. They threw a sheet over our shoulders and buzzed our heads bald in about thirty seconds. When they finished they said, "Now you gotta pay for your haircut."

I saw Benny get that look in his eyes that usually meant somebody was about to get hit. I stepped between Benny and the barbers and said. "How much do we owe you?"

"You can both sing the Mississippi State fight song and we'll call it even."

They handed us a mimeographed copy of the words to the fight song, fortunately we knew the tune. We muddled out way through Hail Dear Old State and paid for the worst haircut I ever got. Ruddy handed us our new Beanies and we gave him two bucks with our thanks. We were ready for our first trip to the Mississippi State Cafeteria.

The four of us walked into the cavernous gothic building that housed the cafeteria. There were exposed oak beams twelve inches square holding up an arched ceiling that must have been 75 feet high. Large ornate chandeliers hung throughout the building providing a warm yellow glow. The air was filled with a mixture of appetizing aromas.

There were three serving lines abutting the far wall, floor to ceiling cathedral windows along the outer wall and tables to seat over a thousand people. We later learned that it was the largest college eating facility in the whole country. The four of us were awe struck and, we must have looked it. A pretty young woman came up to us and said,

"You boys need some help?"

"Yes ma'am," I answered, "we sure do. What's the drill to get something to eat?"

"Well, it's actually pretty simple. You get in one of the three lines over there, grab a tray and go through and choose your food. If you are on the food plan you can get a student plate which includes one meat, one starch and two vegetables, rolls or cornbread, unlimited glasses of milk, coffee, tea or coke. Dessert is included. When you finish, just take your tray to that window over there and put it on the conveyor belt. That's all there is to it."

I thanked the lady and we moved into the nearest line. Sure enough, we had our trays heaped with mountains of wonderful smelling food. We could barely carry them to a table for four. There was the muted humdrum of hundreds of voices, but the building was so large the sound was absorbed in its sheer volume. We dug in and chowed down without much conversation.

"Damn, that was good," Benny exclaimed.

We all agreed that the chow was first class, and I was already looking forward to breakfast.

"What's on our agenda for tonight?" I asked nobody in particular.

"Well, there a couple of options, and if we time it right we can do it all. The first thing you need to do is get your car off the drill field. If it's there after dark they will tow it to the motor barn. After that, we can catch a shuttle bus downtown. The Starkville merchants are throwing a street dance for all of the freshmen. We might meet a couple of honeys. Later on, we ought to go out to the fair grounds for the Oktibbeha County Fair and Livestock show."

"I ain't seen many honeys, where do you suppose they are?

"My guess would be MSCW and Ole Miss." Said Ruddy.

This was disturbing news to say the least. We started toward my car and I said,

"The part about the honeys sounds pretty good, but I may have to pass on the county fair. I don't have much for chicken judging."

"Believe me there is a little more available than the blue ribbons for baking. I know some guys that went last year and they said we shouldn't miss it." Ruddy chimed in.

"Oh well, how dumb can it be?" I said as we all got in my car.

"Where's your back seat?" asked Ruby

"Don't have one, just sit on the floor; it's pretty clean, this is the economy model."

"Economy model or not, at least you got a car."

We finally found an area 5 parking lot. It was totally removed from anything. It took us nearly fifteen minutes to get back to the main part of the campus. We stood in line with a couple of dozen other guys with shaved heads and beanies waiting for our turn on one of the regular stream of shuttle buses. We boarded a bus and were whisked downtown to be disgorged on to Main Street.

Downtown Starkville was comprised of one street three blocks in length. There were two movies, two cafes, a pool hall, Smith and Byars Men's Store, a small hotel and various local merchants. It wasn't Paris, hell, it wasn't even Memphis or Jackson, but it was crowded with hundreds of guys with shaved heads and beanies. What it was not crowded with were coeds. Not a one in sight.

"How in the hell do you have a dance without a single girl. I damn sure ain't going to dance with any of you guys." Benny said.

"Well, they're not depending on Mississippi State coeds, as far as I have been able to ascertain there are only about 350 of them, they may be able to scratch up a few more if some guys fail the ROTC physical and are reassigned. The plan is to bus a couple of hundred freshmen girls over from the W. The buses should be here soon and they don't have to go back until 11:00." Ruby added.

"A couple of hundred, huh, that will make the odds about 10 to 1. I can live with that," replied Benny.

A large cheer began at the end of the downtown area and quickly spread to our end. Five Greyhound Buses filed onto one of the side streets and began to disgorge teenage girls of every description and they all looked great to us. There was the distinct possibility of a stampede and wide spread panic, but a band started playing their rendition of Joe Turner's R&B hit, Honey Hush.

Benny was gone like a shot, and before anyone else could react, he cut one of the prettiest girl out of the herd and was soon dancing in the street. Those five bus loads of girls were gobbled up in nothing flat and the rest of us were on the sidelines looking in. After about five Rock' n' Roll and R&B numbers, the band began to play Smoke Gets In Your Eyes. Benny was a great dancer and slow dancing was his thing; he and his new-found love were grooving in a world of their own.

"Damn, that boy has some moves doesn't he?" said Mickey Braswell.

"Yeah", I said, "Benny has a way with the ladies; they all want to run their fingers through his hair and take him home to Mama."

"He doesn't strike me as the serious type." Ruddy mused.

"Oh, he's serious all right-serious about getting in their pants, and he usually finds a way."

We left Benny to his work and decided to see if we could find where everyone was getting the free cokes. We found the concession stand and took our cokes and walked back to the edge of the dancers crowding Main Street. Soon the level of excitement notched down a level or two and we moved in to ask some girls to dance. Before we knew it 11:00 had come and the band began to pack up their instruments and the girls started moving toward the buses and loading up for the trip back to Columbus twenty miles away. This would be the last time these freshman girls would see 11:00 all year. MSCW had a strict 10:00 pm curfew for freshman and enforced it with the vigor usually associated with maximum security prisons.

There was a lot of "I'll give you a call and maybe we can go out," going on as the buses pulled out and headed for Highway 82. The crowd began to drift away, many guys catching the shuttles back to campus and others getting on the shuttles headed to the Oktibbeha County Fair and Livestock Show. We opted for the fair.

As we boarded the van, Benny said, "I need to borrow your car on Saturday; I've got a date with Jean Miller from Clarksdale."

"That the honey you were with all night?"

"Yeah, she's a pretty cool girl."

"Pretty and cool I'd say."

"Yeah, pretty and cool." Benny said dreamily.

"Sure, you can use the car. I may catch a ride to the W and scout the place out. You can pick me up when you take her in."

The shuttle stopped in a large gravel parking lot adjacent to the fair grounds. The night was turning a little cooler and there was a touch of fall in the air. The lights from the fairgrounds glowed in the near distance outlining a couple of rides and a Ferris wheel. The sounds of the barkers and the music from the rides and side shows carried across the parking lot. The fall breeze brought the aroma of popcorn, cotton candy and just a touch of cattle shit. Sounded and smelled like every fair in America.

We walked down the midway and took in the sights. We bought some corn dogs and slathered them with mustard while listening to the frantic pleas of the carneys as they tried to lure us in to see everything from the Wild Man of Borneo to the Pygmy cannibals from Panama. The same crap that was on every midway you had ever walked down.

We noticed a large number of guys with goofy shaved heads and maroon beanies hurrying toward a large tent near the end of the midway. We decided to check out the excitement. There was a long line waiting to get in the tent and a big sign read:

COME SEE THE MAN WITH THE CAST IRON STOMACH. HE EATS ANYTHING!

"What'ya think?" I said. "Think it's worth fifty cents?"

"Gotta be." Ruddy replied, "This may be the bargain of a lifetime."

So the four of us and about a hundred other guys, paid our fifty cents and filed into the tent. There was a stage set up at the end of the tent with a string bean of a man dressed in an Uncle Sam looking outfit sitting in a big chair with a sign identifying his as "Gerry the Geek"

Gerry must have been close to seven feet tall and would have made Abe Lincoln look like Paul Newman. He was just country ugly. A man dressed in an Irish green suit with yellow socks, spats, bowtie and a yellow bowler hat came on the stage and waved for the crowd to be quiet.

"Ladies and Gentlemen, may I have your undivided attention. Tonight you are going to be astounded by the evening's events. You will be amazed and will not believe your eyes, for tonight you are going to witness one of nature's truly unique individuals: a man with a stomach made of pure cast-iron. A man that can eat and

175

digest any substance on this planet and suffer no ill effect. In fact, he thrives on eating the bizarre. Ladies and Gentlemen, I give you GERRY THE GEEK."

There was a light sprinkling of applause as Gerry stood up and moved to the front of the stage and the man in green said,

"Gerry is ready to have his evening meal, and tonight he has chosen for his appetizer a brand new Brillo Pad. He will enjoy a quart of Quaker State Motor Oil with his Brillo Pad."

A woman dressed in a cocktail waitress uniform entered the stage carrying a tray with a Box of Brillo Pads and a quart can of Quaker State motor oil, neither had been opened. The man in green invited one of the spectators up to verify that neither of the treats had been tampered with. The student confirmed their authenticity.

Gerry pulled out a church key and opened the can of motor oil and poured it into a large glass. It was a pale yellow and he held it up for the crowd to see. He then opened the box of Brillo Pads, carefully removed one, and sat it on a saucer which again he held up for the crowd to see. The crowd was hushed with expectation.

Gerry calmly began taking bites out of the Brillo Pad and gulping large swallows of motor oil. He chewed up the entire pad and finished off the glass of oil. Gerry returned to his seat, and the woman removed the tray and exited stage left.

"Well, I'll just be damned," Ruddy said. "That beats all I've ever seen."

"I'd hate to be around when he takes a dump; it must be like a dog trying to pass a peach pit." I said.

The man in the green suit came back on stage and said,

"Tonight Gerry has chosen chicken as his entrée. He will enjoy a bottle of Tabasco Sauce with his dinner."

Gerry rose from his chair and the woman came out with the tray. There was a live chicken in a small cage and a full 16oz bottle of Tabasco Sauce. Let me digress for a moment to talk about

Tabasco Sauce, the hottest substance available in the South. It was made in South Louisiana and should have come with a skull and crossbones on the label. A couple of drops would handle any dish; a 16oz bottle was a lifetime supply. Again the man in green invited a student to check it out and again all was kosher. Gerry broke the seal on the Tabasco, pulled the little plastic cap off and poured a full glass of the red hot sauce.

He then pulled the live chicken from the little cage, grabbed it by the feet and began eating it head first. Head, feathers, blood, beak, and little yellow feet. He polished off the whole bird and chased it with the entire glass of Tabasco sauce. Gerry, let out a deep rumble of a burp, wiped the blood from his face and returned to his chair. The woman and the tray exited stage left.

The crowd had grown completely quiet about half way through the chicken and was still in a state of shock and awe. The temperature in the tent had risen by about ten degrees and the air was suffused with sweat, chicken odors and cigarette smoke. The man in the green suit returned to the stage and said,

"Like everyone else, Gerry enjoys a dessert with his meals. Tonight he is having a 100 Watt light bulb and a cup of his own hot urine to aid his digestion."

Gerry moved to the front of the stage, the woman with the tray reappeared and the student made the authentication. He took a deep smell of the cup of hot urine and agreed that it was indeed piss of some sort. Gerry was ready to go. He stepped up to the tray, ate the glass portion of the light bulb and began to sip on the cup of hot piss, smacking his lips in appreciation.

The man in green came in a said, "Ladies and Gentlemen you have just witnessed one of the true freaks of nature. GERRY THE GEEK! Let's give him a big round of applause."

We began to file out into the much cooler night air and Benny said, "You gotta know that Gerry is not long for this world. His stomach must be a total disaster area."

"Yeah, well, you have to admit it was well worth fifty cents." I said.

"Maybe the biggest bargain of my life. I wonder what's next?" added Ruddy.

"It'll be hard to top Gerry." Said Mickey.

As events progressed, Mickey's prediction was quickly proven to be in serious error. The next tent held a spectacle that made Gerry look like he should be on the Ed Sullivan Show. We followed the crowd leaving Gerry the Geek to a tent next door where a man dressed in a red suit with purple trim was haranguing a crowd of young men with eager expressions on their collective faces. We stepped into the back of the crowd and tuned into the message.

The message was pretty simple. The man in red was suggesting that if we paid fifty cents, we could come in and enjoy the voluptuous charms of Miss Kitty, the best stripper in all of America. He waxed eloquent as he described Miss Kitty's many physical charms and finally said,

"Gentlemen, I don't expect you to take my word for Miss Kitty, let's just bring the lady herself out to meet you. I present to you the beautiful and charming Miss Kitty."

With that introduction, there was the scratchy rendition of some serious bump and grind music and a vision of loveliness wearing a brocade robe and high heels pranced on to the dais. Now Benny and I were not exactly rookies in this stripper business. My parents had taken us to see Ole Miss play in the Sugar Bowl and we had managed to escape parental supervision long enough to visit Bourbon Street and take in the sights. We had paid a ten dollar cover charge to see the famous Chris Owens take it off down to a G string and pasties. We both wished we had our ten dollars back. We had seen more at the Drive-In Movie. We were skeptical.

Miss Kitty did her bump and grind routine for a few minutes and the man in red said,

"Miss Kitty, give the boys a little preview of what they will see inside."

With that, Miss Kitty opened her robe and gave us all a shot of her birthday suit. It was barely a peek, but it served its purpose. A couple of hundred scholars lined up to pay fifty cents to see more of Miss Kitty. The four of us were included in the rush, what the hell, for fifty cents you couldn't get hurt too bad.

The tent was brightly lit and all was focused on a small stage that was roped off like a boxing ring. The man in red came on to the stage and announced,

"Gentlemen, you are about to enjoy a show that has received rave reviews in all of the major world capitals. I present to you a star of stage, film and television, Miss Kitty Katt."

The bump and grind music started backstage and Miss Kitty strutted across the stage. She was wearing a series of translucent veils that revealed the general shape of her body, but hid the real details. The general shape was outstanding. After a couple of circuits of the stage she let one of the veils slip to the floor and a roar of lustful exuberance rose from the crowd like a primeval mating call.

Miss Kitty caught the discarded veil with the toe of her high-heel shoe and kicked it high above the cheering crowd. There was a fight for the veil that all most came to fists, but two very large Carney workers moved quickly to restore decorum. With each circuit of the stage Miss Kitty lost another veil and either kicked it or tossed it to the crowd. Expectation and excitement leapt and the distinct musty odor of testosterone filled the dank air. Finally there was but one long veil strategically covering Miss Kitty.

This last impediment to carnal satisfaction soon hit the floor and the crowd growled in approval. At this point I, for the first time, understood the thin line that separates a crowd from a mob. We were running close to that line. Miss Kitty could sense this and her nipples hardened and she began to move with a sensuousness that had been missing from the first part of her performance. She was getting into it.

Miss Kitty may have been close to forty and it was clear that she had a great many miles on her odometer, she sagged a bit here and there, but she had one major thing going for her: tonight she was the only game in town. She was the queen of Starkville, Mississippi.

Never missing a bump or a grind she stepped over the barrier ropes and with one hand holding the rope she reached down and slipped a pair of horn rim glasses from a pimply faced guy in the first row. Slinking back across the ropes she began to caress the glasses all over her body and finally inserted them in that glorious place that houses all of man's desire. She finally withdrew the spectacles and tossed them back to the owner who caught them in mid air as if they were relics of the true cross. I suspect he treasures them to this day.

This resulted in a near riot of guys hurling personal items to the stage. Everything from fountain pens to tennis shoes. One might wonder about the maximum volume Miss Kitty might be able to accommodate. She ignored the fusillade of possible dildos and retreated back stage. The crowd pleaded for an encore, chanting the name, MISS KITTY, MISS KITTY, MISS KITTY.

Instead of Miss Kitty, the man in red returned with the microphone. Gesturing for quiet he said,

"Fellows, as I promised, you have seen the Queen of The Strippers and I hope you are pleased."

A swelling wave of animal instinct rose with a background chorus of MISS KITTY, MISS KITTY, and MISS KITTY.

The man in red continued, "Well boys, if you like the first act, you're going to love the second one. Miss Kitty will demonstrate her amazing ability to control all parts of her body, especially those that can provide so much pleasure to men. We are going to take a ten-minute intermission and you must leave the tent. There will be an additional fifty cent admission to the second act."

This announcement was greeted by an angry snarl of disapproval.

Again signaling for quiet, the man in red said, "Now, now fellows, don't jump to the wrong conclusion, all funds garnered by the second act are donated to Miss Kitty's retirement fund. While our lady has many good years to continue to pursue her career, girls must prepare for the future. After all, as they say in the song, Diamonds Are A Girl's Best Friend. Let's get Miss Kitty some diamonds."

The announcement of Miss Kitty's retirement performance seemed to calm the crowd and we all filed from the tent. Once outside Ruddy said.

"I thought it would be hard to get more entertainment and education from fifty cents than Gerry the Geek, but I do believe Miss Kitty has raised the bar."

"I'd have to boil those glasses if they were mine; there's no telling what sort of organism might be lurking inside Miss Kitty." Benny said.

"Benny, that's a very cynical attitude to take toward a fair maiden like Miss Kitty. I am shocked by your crass mistrust."

"Shocked as you may be, I'll bet you wouldn't want your glasses in her plumbing."

The man in red reappeared and said that the box office was open for the second act and almost the entire crowd lined up to see Miss Kitty's follow up performance. We resumed our positions in the tent, but we were able to elbow our way near to the front.

The lights went on and the man in red came on stage with a galvanized pail in his hand. He looked into the crowd and began. "Gentlemen, Miss Kitty is going to demonstrate the amazing physical control that has made her a favorite on five continents. I have here in my bucket two dozen ping pong balls."

He took one of the balls and dropped it to the stage and grabbed in on the rebound and said,

"Before the night is done, twenty-four of you lucky fellows will have the opportunity to own a treasured relic of Miss Kitty's sensual prowess. Let's go on with the show!"

The music came on, but instead of the bump and grind it was the 1812 Overture. As the French approached the Russian capital, Miss Kitty began inserting ping pong balls in her most strategic orifice. Soon the weapon was fully loaded and Miss Kitty moved to the edge of the stage and faced the crowd.

As the bells began to toll and the cannons blasted away, Miss Kitty began to expel ping pong balls into the crowd. Having moved to the front of the tent assured that we would not get a chance to own a memento of the evening. The balls were flying at least twenty- five feet into the back of the tent. A melee of pushing, shoving, and cursing young men fought savagely for a relic of Miss Kitty's performance.

It took the two carneys and several backups to restore order. Miss Kitty took a bow to a thunder of applause and left the stage waving goodbye. The man in red returned.

"Gentlemen that concludes our show for this evening, however, if any of would like to meet Miss Kitty in person she will be willing to spend up to fifteen minutes with you in private. If you have an interest in having a personal session with Miss Kitty please see me after the show. Good night and I hope you have enjoyed our production."

We were back on the midway trying to determine our next move. Ruddy said, "I think I have had about all I can enjoy for one night; I'm headed to Old Main."

Mickey had a faraway look on his face and said,

"I think I might try my hand with a private session with Miss Kitty, I may want to make a further contribution to her retirement fund."

I laughed and said, "Benny and I had a private session with Miss Kitty's look-alike during National Guard camp this summer, it was six minutes of pure bliss. Good Luck!"

Without much more conversation we caught the shuttle back to campus and walked up the stairs to our third-floor room. We said good night to Ruddy and opened our door and pulled the light string. The room was filled with a dim yellow glow; it was at best, a twenty five watt bulb. Our rat roomie was sitting on Benny's bed.

"Benny, I think we got a pet. Why don't you encourage him to get in his crack in the wall and go to bed?"

"Well, if we are going to keep him we might as well give him a name. How about Malcolm, he reminds me of that little fink Malcolm Maskawitz from Boy Scout camp, remember him?"

"Yeah, he does look like Maskawitz, hope he has a better disposition. "

We stripped down to our shorts and took our dop kits to the head. We did our evening toilette and returned to our room. We had left the windows open and the room had cooled to a point of being habitable. We moved our guns out of the beds and put them underneath. Malcolm sat in the corner taking the whole scene in. Benny pulled the light cord and the room was filled with the defused light of the closed cafeteria and other campus lighting.

"What did you think of our first day at school?" Benny asked.

"Pretty damn educational I'd say."

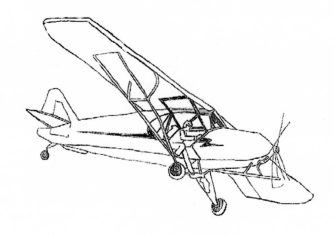

Geronimo

The Mississippi State band was marching off Scott Field playing Hail Dear Old State. It was half time at Homecoming and State was leading Memphis State 21-7. The public address announcer boomed across the stadium.

"Ladies and gentlemen, I call your attention to the airplane circling high above the stadium. There will be four members of the Mississippi State Parachute team jumping and landing on the fifty-yard line."

Four tiny figures exited the airplane and fell toward earth at heart stopping speed. At what seemed the last possible minute, all four parachutes blossomed open and the quartet landed within yards of the mid field stripe. All four made a stand up landing.

"These daring young men recently won the Colligate Free Fall Competition in Orange New Jersey; let's give them a rousing Bulldog welcome!"

There was a perfunctory round of applause as the four jumpers gathered their canopies and exited field left. The leader of the team was my very own roommate, Benny Bowman. Benny and I had grown up in Cumberland, a small town in the Mississippi Delta, and had shared almost all of our youth together. The only thing that we didn't do together was sport parachuting.

During the summer between the 10th and 11th grades, Benny ordered a surplus Army parachute from an advertisement in Argosy magazine. In due time this relic of WWII arrived and we picked it up at the local bus station. We couldn't wait to get it to Benny's garage workshop and see just what we had. What we had was not very impressive. An olive drab bundle about the size of an Army backpack

"Okay, now that you've got it, what do we do next?" I asked.

"Let's go out to the airport and talk to Billy Exeter. I'll bet he'll take me up."

'Oh, for ten bucks Exeter would take Babe the Blue Ox up. Just what to you plan to do when he gets you up there?"

"Jump out."

"I was afraid you were going to say that."

Benny's Dad was letting him use one of the old lumber yard pickup trucks and we piled the package in the back and headed for the little airport on the edge of town. In the Delta it was hard to see exactly where the cotton fields ended and civilization began. Since WWII, the demand for fiber was at an all time high and the farmer's were planting every available acre. From ground level the airport seemed to be a small group of buildings in a huge cotton field.

The single grass runway had cotton on three sides with a small quonset type hanger and office at the other. We parked next to the office, grabbed the parachute and went looking for Billy Exeter, airport owner, chief pilot, mechanic, crop duster, flight instructor and former P51 Mustang pilot. Billy lived in the back room of his hanger and was constantly short of cash. He was for hire.

We entered the hanger through the big sliding doors and walked toward a figure dressed in a greasy flight suit with his head hidden inside the back seat of a Stearman Biplane.

"Hey Billy, what's up?" Benny yelled.

From deep inside the fuselage of the old biplane a muffled voice said,

"I can't find the end of this goddamn control wire. I know it's gotta be somewhere in here, but damned if I can find it."

Exeter pulled himself out of the airplane and wiped his hands on a greasy towel.

"What can I do for you guys?"

"My parachute arrived today," Benny replied, "and you can take me up to jump it."

"That it you're holding?"

"Yeah that's it."

"Bring it over to my work bench and let's take a look," Exeter said, then added,

"Bowman, that's not an airborne main chute. It looks like an Air Force reserve."

"Airborne, Air Force, what the hell, a parachute's a parachute and I'm ready to go."

"Bowman, you don't have shit for sense. You could break your damn neck in that thing."

"Billy, you made a parachute jump and you didn't break your neck."

"Yeah, I jumped all right. I had a ME 109 taking my plane apart with cannon fire. I never jumped out of a fully functioning aircraft, you can bet your ass on that."

"Well, I want to do it, you gonna take me up?"

"If you got $10 to invest in this little exercise in lunacy, I'm your man. Get that piece of shit parachute on and meet me out by the other Stearman, it's got about a half load of cotton poison in the hopper, but I can probably get it off the ground. You don't weigh that much."

That left Benny and me to puzzle through trying to figure out how in the dickens to get him strapped into the chute. You might think that it would be intuitive, but there were buckles and straps all over the place. We finally worked it out, or at least we hoped we'd worked it out. At any rate, Benny was wearing the thing and it was securely fastened to him in several different areas. He was ready to go.

Billy Exeter took one look at Benny and sighed deeply,

187

"Bowman, if you jump with that thing upside down you're going to rupture yourself and probably land on your head. Let me at least show you how to get in the rigging."

Billy helped Benny get the chute on right side up and tightened all of the straps and buckles.

"By the way, that thingamajig near your chest is called a D ring. It'd be a good idea to pull that sometime before you actually hit the ground. There is some small amount of hope that the canopy will deploy, though I wouldn't really count on it. According to that tag, this baby was packed in France in 1945. God only knows what will come out, hopefully the canopy, but probably someone's laundry."

"Whatever," Benny muttered. "Let's do it."

Benny climbed into the backseat of the bright yellow crop duster. Billy revved the big radial engine and they begin to roll down the grass runway. The plane seemed to be laboring a bit, but soon they were airborne and gaining altitude rapidly. In about five minutes Billy leveled off and begin to make a wide circle of the airport.

Soon a tiny speck separated from the circling plane and plunged toward the adjacent cotton field. At what seemed to be the last moment, there was a loud pop and, lo and behold, the chute blossomed like a big white sail. Benny floated down and disappeared into the chest high cotton. The only thing that I could see was the billowing parachute as it flapped in the breeze.

Benny surfaced in the sea of green and began gathering up the now deflated canopy and walking slowly toward the runway. Billy landed the Stearman and taxied over near me and killed the engine. Benny walked up with a huge grin and said,

"Man, what a rush. That was the best thing I've ever done. Let's do it again."

"Bowman, having cheated death once this afternoon, I might suggest you call it a day and go try to figure out how to repack that rag," Billy commented.

"Yeah, there is that." Benny replied. "I hadn't thought about how to repack it; It looks like it will never go back into that little bag."

"Let's take this over to the Armory and ask Maggio what to do." I suggested.

Sergeant Pauli Maggio was the full time employee of the Mississippi National Guard,, as well as our Company E first sergeant. He and our Company Commander, Captain James Millstone served together as NCO's in the 502nd Parachute Infantry Regiment of the 101st Airborne Division.

Both had jumped into Normandy and Holland and had been encircled at Bastogne during the Battle of the Bulge. Millstone had received a battlefield Commission, two Silver Stars and the DSM. Maggio had about the same decorations. He would know all about parachutes.

The Cumberland armory was adjacent to the Campus of Bayou State Teacher's College on the western edge of town. It was cavernous building with offices and equipment storage in the front and a large open space the size of your average gym in the back. Sgt. Maggio's office was the only air conditioned room in the building and he was sitting behind his army issue metal desk when we came through the door hauling the parachute along.

He looked up from his newspaper and said,

"What have I done to merit a visit from you two super troopers?"

"We need your help and advice," Benny replied.

"Advice I can guarantee you, help may be conditional. What's up?"

"I just received the parachute that I ordered and Billy Exeter took me up and I jumped over the airport. It was the most exciting thing I've ever done."

"Is that the chute?" asked Maggio. "Let me take a look at it."

Benny heaved the piled -up chute up on a nearby table and Maggio got up from behind his desk and came over to look. He began checking out the whole package, paying particular attention to a tag bearing the date 1945.

"Do you idiots have any idea when this thing was packed? How about 1945. It has been sitting in some warehouse for nearly ten years. I'm amazed it opened this morning. I can't believe you were stupid enough to jump it. I am not amazed that Exeter was stupid enough to take you up. He just hasn't been right since he got out that German prison camp. "

"Darn, Sarge, we thought you would be pleased to see us take some initiative to further our military skills," I said.

"Larch, don't tell me you are planning to take an active part in this insanity?"

"Only in a support role, I'm not going to jump, you can depend on that." I assured him.

"Good, there may some hope for you yet, as far Bowman here, he may be too far gone."

Maggio was shaking his head as he returned to his desk and leaned back in his swivel chair. He thought for a while and finally he said,

"Look guys, I really can understand why you want to do this as crazy as it sounds. When I was your age I volunteered for airborne training and had made my first jump before I turned 18. You'll notice that I said "airborne training", that makes a major difference in our circumstances. Jumping can be reduced to an acceptable level of risk with the proper training and experience, but to take a ten year old parachute up and jump is just plain nuts. Does your old man know about this?"

"Well, sorta. I told him what I planned to do and he mumbled something like, that's nice, be careful or something similar. He never really listens, but he'll get over it. That's how I got in the Guard to start with."

"Hmm," mused Maggio.

"Okay, Bowman, I'm not going to help you repack that relic, nor am I going to have anything to do with any more jumping until you get some training. What I will do is recommend to the CO that you be sent to jump school and riggers school this summer. We can send a couple of guys off for specialized training and I guess you'll do as well as anyone, but you gotta promise that you won't jump again till you get back. Now throw that piece of crap away and get outta my office."

Benny did indeed go to jump school that summer as well as becoming a master parachute rigger. The following year he made over 50 jumps, including a dozen or so free falls. By the time we got to Mississippi State he was considered to be an expert jumper and founded the MSU Sports Parachuting Club that won the Nationals.

The Sunday following the Homecoming game, which by the way State won 42-14, Benny and I were laying around our room shooting the bull when I decided that I wanted to try a jump. I had been watching Benny for over three years and it had never occurred to me to do it. It just looked like it might be a lot of fun when they floated down and gently landed on the fifty-yard line.

"You know what I've been thinking?" I said.

Benny looked up from his latest issue of MAD and said.

"I hesitate to ask, but tell me anyway."

"I've decided that I want to make a jump."

Later I learned that Benny had been waiting to hear these words for three years, and I have to admit he played it absolutely cool. He dangled the bait, but did not set the hook.

"You remember what Sgt. Maggio told me that first day I jumped?" he asked.

"You mean that speech about jumping being a reasonable risk with the proper training, Yeah I do remember it."

Well, that still applies. I've made over 200 jumps and I'm more convinced than ever about proper training. If you want to try it, you'll have to agree to letting me get you to a minimum level of training."

"I wouldn't have it any other way."

"Okay, next time I'm going out to Hamp's you can come along and start picking up on some of the basics. I'll probably go Wednesday afternoon; I get out of class at 3:00 on Wednesday's."

"That's great; I'll plan on tagging along with you and start to get the feel for this thing."

Sure enough, Wednesday rolled around and when I walked into our room about 3:15, Benny was lacing up his jump boots, ready to head to Hamp's little airport. He looked up at me and said,

"You gonna come along? You can watch me pack a few chutes."

"Yeah, that sounds good."

"Grab your combat boots and a sweatshirt; we may try to get you fitted into the harnesses just to familiarize you with the rig."

I picked up my National Guard boots, grabbed a MSU sweatshirt and followed Benny out the door. We walked down the three flights of stairs into the Hull Hall parking lot and threw our stuff into the empty space in back of my car.

It was late October and the Mississippi State campus was awash with gold and red scattered all over the green expanse of the lawns and clinging determinedly to the large oaks that were everywhere. Fall had always been my favorite time of the year: hunting and football beckoned, and the cool air was diffused with the acrid aroma of burning leaves and cotton seed waste. All was well and I looked forward to starting my extensive parachute training on such a beautiful day.

We pulled into the little local airport and parked the car near a low-ceilinged building with a sign that said, Mississippi State Sport

Parachuting Club. It seemed odd to me that in the two years we had been at State, I had never even visited the airport, not to mention the club that Benny had founded. I actually felt a little embarrassed.

We hauled our gear into the building which was dominated by a very long, very smooth, hardwood table about five feet wide. Benny told me to hang my boots and sweatshirt on a hook on the wall and come with him to the storeroom at the other end of the long low building. Benny opened a locked closet door and started rummaging through a pile of parachute packs. He finally found what he was looking for and grabbed a pack and re-locked the door.

He guided me back to the long hardwood table and flopped the pack near one end. He began to unhook and unlace a variety of fasteners and soon he was pulling an olive drab silk canopy out of he pack and smoothing it out on the rigging table.

"That looks like its regular Army issue," I said.

"It is, I brought a bunch of surplus 35 -foot airborne main chutes and 28 foot reserves back from Fort Bragg when I finished my summer training. Thought I would pick one and show you how it's packed. '

Benny began smoothing and folding the canopy into a tight bundle, carefully placing the little lines in their proper place.

"These are called suspension lines" he said, pointing to one of the small ropelike lines. They connect to these canvas belts called risers. You use them to control the direction of your descent. Got that?"

"Sure," I replied, despite the fact that I had no idea what he was talking about.

When he completed packing the chute, he motioned me over and said.

"Get your boots and sweatshirt on and we'll get you set up with this chute so you can begin to get comfortable with the weight and balance."

As soon as I was outfitted with the main chute pack, Benny said,

"I want you to jog around the building to get things settled in and we'll do one more round of tightening everything up. You need to have a pretty good range of motion, but no loose fittings."

I didn't have much problem jogging since my lower body was not involved with the parachute. I completed the circuit of the building and came back in. Benny was talking to one of the club members and turned to me and said,

"You might as well try on the reserve chute while we're at it. Come over and stand on this box and we'll get you set up."

The reserve chute buckled and hooked on to the shoulder straps of the main pack and really didn't seem all that awkward, just a little more weight. I jumped up and down to get everything settled in and said,

"This is a real load, I can't believe paratroopers have to carry all their gear, weapons and ammo when they jump, I'm surprised they can crawl on to the airplane."

"Yeah, it's a struggle, but you gotta have all that stuff when you hit a hot landing zone." Benny replied, and added, "While we're on the subject of landing there are a couple of things that are real important."

I nodded in agreement and said,

"You have my full attention."

"You are going to use a static line to open your chute and in 99 out of 100 cases there won't be a need to worry about your reserve, but should your main canopy either not open or fail to inflate, just pull the D ring on your reserve and you'll be fine."

"One chance in one hundred huh?"

"It's probably a lot better than that, I've made hundreds of jumps and have yet to have a problem. Just be aware of what to do if you need it."

"You'll be jumping from about 2500 feet, so I'd try to pull the D Ring within the first 10 seconds."

"Ten seconds, huh?"

Well, hell, how dangerous can this be? Sounds like the odds are in my favor.

"There are a couple of other things to bear in mind, Benny added, Don't look straight down after your chute opens, cause everything looks the same from 2500 feet as it does from 50 feet. Keep your eye on the horizon to judge your altitude. Glance down occasionally to make sure you're not headed for water or trees, but mainly watch the horizon."

"Water or trees, huh?"

Yeah, you can guide the chute by pulling on the risers. You'll always be moving in the direction that you're facing; there is an open gore in the back of the chute that will assure this. If you want to go to the right pull the right riser, left pull the left riser. You'll be amazed at how much control you have."

"What the hell is an open gore?" I asked.

"We cut a panel out of the back of the chute to allow air to escape during your descent. This moves the canopy in the direction opposite the missing panel."

"Does this make the chute come down faster?" I asked.

"Not appreciably, it's well worth the increased speed of descent to gain the control. C'mon outside and let's try to learn to make a rolling landing."

I waddled out the door following Benny. We walked over to a 55-gallon oil drum with a wooden box beside it.

"Climb up on the top of that oil drum and jump off." Benny instructed.

With some small difficulty, I managed to clamber on to the oil drum. I jumped off and landed stiff legged and upright.

"That was a perfect example how not to land. Do that and you'll drive your legs up into your chest cavity and that ain't a good thing. Watch me now."

Benny climbed atop the drum and jumped off. Just as his feet hit the ground; he folded his legs, twisted his body and did a perfect roll on the grass."

"When you roll like that your body spreads the shock of impact and allows your legs and torso to absorb most of it. Much safer and a hell of a lot more comfortable. Now give it another try."

I did the maneuver again, this time rolling just as Benny had. It felt natural and instinctive. Clearly the way to do it.

"Well, that completes your extensive pre-jump training, Ready to go?"

"Go where?" I asked.

"Go up and jump. You're as ready as you'll ever be."

"Go up and jump right now?"

Out of the corner of my eye I saw a group of guys intently watching this little tableau play out. They were all grinning like a herd of jackasses eating briars. This little assembly included damn near everyone I knew at Mississippi State. They stared at me expectantly.

There is a gland present in every young man that tells him that he is bullet proof. It also will not allow him to back down, even in the face of total stupidity. This gland gave me a large squirt of adrenalin and I turned to Benny and said,

"Well, why not? Let's do it."

196

"Roger that" he said, "Follow me to the flight line. We should be all ready to go."

We walked over to a two-seat red Aeronca Chief. The little plane had front and back seats and Benny climbed into the back seat and told me to hook my static line to the front seat floor bracket. I noticed that the front door had been removed to make it easier and to get in and out.   I hooked it up and awaited further instructions.

"Well, get in the damn plane, don't just stand there." Benny growled.

"What's got a bug up your ass?" I asked.

"It's not important; these idiots filled the damn gas tank full."

"I would think that would be a good idea."

"It would be if we were going somewhere, but it makes us a little overloaded."

"Is that going to be a problem?"

"I doubt it; we can probably still take off."

"Probably huh?"

"Just get in the damn plane and let me worry about flying it. At least you've got a parachute if anything happens. I'll have to ride this little mother down."

"Thanks, Benny, I feel a whole lot better." I said, and tried to climb into the front seat. I say tried, because there was no way that six- feet two, two-hundred-and -twenty five-pound body with two parachutes was going to fit in that little front seat. Aid from the ground crew didn't help. I just could not get in.

"Aw shit," Benny mumbled under his breath, "Just put one of your feet on the little step and hold on to the wings struts, it'll be easier to exit the plane from out there."

I placed my left foot on a small strip of metal about 1" by 6" and my right foot dangled in space. I grabbed a wing strut with both hands and let my butt rest on the front seat. I was more out than in, but it didn't feel all that awkward. I could do this.

Benny revved the little 65 hp engine and we began to roll down the grass airstrip. I had not bothered to pay much attention to the runway, but all of a sudden it became my number one concern. It looked to be several hundred yards long and there was a line of large oak trees at the end.

We gained ground speed and about half way down the strip I saw Benny pull back on the stick. Nothing happened. As we continued to gain ground speed we began to bounce along, each bounce a little longer and higher than the last. We had covered about three quarters of the length of the strip and the oaks began to loom threateningly as we sped toward them. I stuck my head in and hollered at Benny.

"Are we going to make it? I shouted.

"Hell, I hope so." Benny replied.

"Hope so, huh?"

The bouncing quit and we were airborne, the only problem is we were about six feet off the ground and fast approaching forty-foot oak trees. This was the first of several crucial decision that I was forced to make in the next twenty minutes. I could unhook my static line and roll out of the airplane before it hit the trees and probably not sustain life threatening injury. Some broken bones and such, but I would not die in the fire that would surely engulf the little plane when it hit the trees, or I could take a chance that Benny could pull out the take-off. I bet on Benny.

To this day, I have no idea how he managed it. There was a blur of green, the sound of branches breaking and before I knew it we were climbing over the small grove of trees and steadily gaining altitude. I was amazed and grateful. Jumping would be a snap now, or so I thought.

I had flown enough with Benny in small airplanes to have some sense of how things oughta be. There was definitely something wrong with this flight. For one thing the little engine was laboring with all of its might to gain each foot of altitude and secondly, we were flying with our nose up rather than level. I realized that Benny was struggling to prevent a stall.

Later, I learned that the climb rate of a fully loaded Aeronca was 370 feet per minute. It would normally take us minutes to reach 2500 feet. We had been up for at least 10 minutes and I bet we were still less than 1000 feet. This was going to take a while.

We labored along for another ten minutes or so and Benny tapped me on the shoulder and shouted above the engine noise,

I'm gonna hand you a roll of toilet paper, I want you to throw it out and hold on to the loose end. I'm gonna bank the plane and watch it stream to see the direction of the winds. Hang on when I bank, O.K.?"

"O.K." I shouted and took the roll he offered. I held the loose end and tossed the roll into the airstream and Benny banked the plane to the right. This brought about the second "Aw, Shit" moment of the flight. Now the plane was flying with one wing up and one wing down. I was no longer perched on the seat and little step, but was hanging on the wing struts dragging the plane down. I wrapped my legs around the bottom of the struts and hung on for dear life. It was clear to me that we could not maintain altitude it this position. Benny agreed and was shouting at me to let go. The choice was clear. Hang on we both die in a fiery crash, or let go and take my chances.

I decided to let go, but first I made what may have been the first sincere prayer of my young life. I said,

"God, I'm not going to start making promises in the face of probable death, but anything you can do for me between here and the ground will be greatly appreciated."

I let go. I plunged into space and felt a strong jerk from my back and noticed that I was no longer falling to earth, but I seemed to be floating down. I looked up and to my surprise and everlasting gratitude saw the large camo canopy fully filled and fully functional."

The next thirty seconds or so made the entire experience worth the effort. There is no sensation that I have ever experienced to compare with floating down in a parachute. There was no sound, just the faint hiss of air rushing by my ears. I could see forever. There was a feeling of being weightless. All of my senses were acutely tuned. Adrenalin is a wonderful thing.

My euphoria was soon interrupted by the thought that I was eventually going to hit the ground. I decided to take a look straight down to see if there were any obstacles that needed to be avoided. Bad Idea!

I hit the ground in the exact wrong position. My legs crumpled under me and I hit face first in the pasture. I then bounced back and landed on my left ankle. I lay there assessing whether or not I was dead and finally decided that miraculously I had survived the worst landing in the history of parachuting.

It took a moment to feel the warm liquid running down my face and to taste the coppery flavor or my own blood. I had broken my nose again. I tried to sit up and reach into the back pocket of my jeans to get my handkerchief when I noticed a dull throbbing in my left ankle. I had injured that ankle bad enough to prevent me from walking on for State's football team, and I had done it again.

While I was sitting in the middle of the pasture taking a physical inventory, the canopy was filling with the wind and tugging against me. I realized that I had to gather it up and keep it from dragging me off. As I tried to regain my feet I heard an approaching roar and looked up just in time to see the little red Aeronca heading straight for me about six feet off the ground.

I flattened against the pasture as the little red plane screamed overhead. Benny pulled up like a crop duster and made a wide 360-degree turn and came roaring back, again six feet off the ground. I stayed flat on my back and gave him the international finger sign as he made another wide turn and headed back.

It was clear to me that I would not be able to stand up and get my aching ass out of the pasture until Benny decided I had not killed myself and returned to Hamp's airport. While he was making his third pass over my head I picked up several dried cow turds and threw them into his path. The turds hit the prop and powdered all over the cockpit. Benny seemed to get the signal and flew off toward the field.

I managed to gain my feet in spite of my aching ankle, which was actually starting to feel a little better. My nose had stopped bleeding and all in all I was in pretty good shape. I started across the pasture headed in the same direction that Benny had taken. At the first fence line I realized that while I was carrying my deflated canopy, I was still harnessed up with the reserve chute and the empty main back pack. I peeled out of the whole rig, made a pile and threw it across the barbed wire fence.

This routine continued for about a half mile when I finally came to a black-topped road that I figured would take me to Highway 82 which in turn would get me back to Hamp's. I had walked maybe a quarter of a mile when I saw my car approaching, Benny at the wheel. He stopped and I threw the parachute gear in the back seat space and we headed to Hamp's.

"Well, that was something less than a textbook first jump." Benny said.

"Yeah," I agreed, "it's a miracle you didn't kill us both in that little red piece of crap."

"I'll have to admit there were a few tense moments. By the way, I wish I had a picture of your exit. It would be the perfect example of how not to do it."

"Unless you need to start a new trend having your jumpers hanging on the wing struts, I can't imagine who you would have the balls to show it to. If I were you, I would hope no one saw the whole debacle."

"You may have a point, by the way, where did all of the blood come from?" Benny asked.

"My broken nose, I made something less than a classic landing. I hurt my ankle too, but it seems to be okay now."

"Well, we'll drop your chutes off at the club house and meet the guys at the Cross Roads. You could use a beer or two."

We ditched the chutes in the club house and headed back to Highway 82 and a local beer joint known as the Cross Roads because it was located at the intersection of Highways 82 and 45, just across the Oktibbeha/Lowndes county line. The Cross Roads was at this time the largest retail outlet for beer in the US. It was nine miles from the Mississippi State Campus and the first beer available in Lowndes County.

It was always difficult to explain Mississippi's liquor laws prior to the legalization of alcohol in the late sixties. The state was officially dry, but beer sales were allowed on a county-option basis. Whiskey was illegal in every county, but readily available in all the river counties on the western side of the state and the entire Gulf Coast. They had liquor stores and could serve it by the drink.

It was also available in private clubs in most of the larger counties and there were bootleggers operating openly everywhere. The State taxed all alcohol sales even though they were technically illegal. This was done by the State Tax Commissioner on a fee/commission basis and he was the highest paid official in the United States. You really had to be there to understand this tangled mess.

The Cross Roads understood it perfectly and there was a literal mountain of empty steel and aluminum beer cans about the size of the Matterhorn behind the joint. I was never much of a beer drinker, and Benny might have one or two, but really didn't much care one way or the other. I suggested that we take a quick detour north on Highway 45 and get a couple of pints of Early Times at the Woodpile. We pulled off of 45 onto a little black top road and headed back West.

We were driving straight into the setting sun and the pastures and occasional cotton field were bathed in the purples, pinks and corals of what promised to be a spectacular sunset. There was a hint of frost in the evening air and the world seemed at peace. We pulled in behind the little sharecropper's shack with the wood stacked on the front porch and hit the horn a couple of toots. Almost instantly an old black man came out the back door of the shack with a wide smile on his face.

"How ya doin' Mista Tom, hadn't seen you this week." He said.

"I'm fine Willie, how you doin'?"

"If I wuz doin' any better, I'd be gone to glory. What's yo' pleasure today?"

That was sort of a rhetorical question on Willie's part. The Woodpile's selection was pretty simple. They had half pints of Early Times at $1.05 and Pints at $1.95 and that was it.

"Well have a couple of pints," I said and handed Willie $4.00 and told him to keep the change. He thanked me and we headed back to the Cross Roads. We pulled into the huge gravel parking lot just as the sun was dipping below the horizon. The large wooden building had windows across the front and we could see it was about half full of students.

We walked in the front door and were immediately immersed in the aroma of fried food, stale beer and cigarette smoke. The dim lighting was supplied mainly by a host of beer signs and blinking pinball machines. Gambling was also illegal in Mississippi but in certain areas the local sheriff looked the other way. Pinball machines paid off and you could place a bet on the football cards. Like I said, you had to live there to hope to understand it.

We saw our friends sitting at a long table with ten or so wooden chairs. They were all drinking draft beer and there were a couple of huge pitchers of draft on the table. A couple of large platters of French fries were being passed around. I edged up to the long bar and ordered ice and water and carried it over to the table. Benny and I grabbed a seat and he had a beer while I poured about 3 inches of Early Times over some ice.

The group began to break up about 10:00 pm when I was working on the second pint of Bourbon. I decided it was time to eat something and I ordered an open faced steak sandwich with lots of gravy, one of my all time favorites. It would probably be a good idea to get something in my stomach besides bourbon.

Benny and I said goodbye to the last of the beer drinkers and headed back to campus. It was a beautiful cool crisp fall night with a huge full moon. We could have easily driven safely without the headlights. We made the nine miles to our dorm in relative silence, both of us beginning to feel that tiredness that overcomes you when you have had a really good day.

We climbed the three floors to our dorm room and began to undress. Benny went down the hall to take a whiz and I began to unlace my combat boots. I loosened the laces and pulled my left foot out of the boot. I could actually see it balloon to almost twice its normal size and begin to throb with each beat of my heart. I pulled the sock off and my entire lower leg was a montage of blues, greens and purples. It hurt like hell.

By the time Benny made it back to the room I was in intense pain and my foot looked really scary. Benny took one look and said,

"Let's get your ass over to the infirmary right now."

"I'm not sure I can walk on this thing," I said.

"Don't worry, I'll get some help and we'll get you over there."

Benny left to knock on the door across the hall and two of our friends came in and took a look at my leg. They agreed that I needed to go to the infirmary as quickly as we could get there. They helped me down the three flights of stairs and Benny had pulled the car right up to the dorm door. They were soon lugging my ass into the Mississippi State Infirmary.

One of the things we had learned in our five years in the Mississippi National Guard was never, ever, allow yourself to be admitted to an Army Hospital if you were conscious and not on death's door step. Once you were admitted it was absolute hell to ever get out. The longer you stayed, the more danger you were in. The army docs were not the brightest and the best and they welcomed any opportunity to operate on captive patients. You could go in for a common cold and have your leg amputated. The State infirmary had the same reputation.

My damn foot hurt so bad I didn't care where they took me, just get me some relief. Since it was close to midnight, there was a student orderly on the desk. He took me into an examining room and took a look at my foot.

"Damn," he said, "What in the hell did you do to get this?"

Before Benny could reply I said, "I fell down the dorm stairs."

"You must live on the fifteenth floor to do this much damage. I'm gonna admit you and give you some pain killers. Dr. Shortest will be here about nine in the morning to take a look at you."

"Bullshit," Benny said, "Call that lazy son-of-a-bitch and tell him to get his incompetent ass over here right now."

"Man, I can't do that; it really pisses him off if he gets called in after he leaves at five. He'll fire my ass."

"Well my man, you've got a real problem staring you right in the face. You are going to have to decide which you would rather have happen, Shortest chew your ass out, or me beat the living shit out you in the next thirty seconds."

Benny did not make idle threats. He also rarely gave warning that he was about to start swinging. I figured this poor guy had about ten seconds to make a choice or it would be decided for him.

"I've got an idea," I said "tell the old fart that there's a freshman girl that came it needing a pelvic exam. He'll be here like a shot. You can tell him she changed her mind and left just as they hauled me in."

"You know that would probably work, let's give it a go."

Shortest arrived in less than ten minutes and seemed disappointed by the missing freshman girl, but examined my foot with a minimum of bitching. He declared my ankle badly sprained, maybe broken, but would have to wait till morning to get some X-rays to be sure. In the mean time, he put me in a room and elevated my foot in some sort of sling. He gave me four aspirins and remarked that I should have no trouble sleeping considering the alcohol load I was carrying.

Benny stuck around until I started to drift off and told me he would see me in the morning. I slept the sleep of the innocent and thoroughly drugged up. At six the next morning I was taken to X-ray and it was determined that my ankle was not broken, just badly sprained. Painful, but fully recoverable.

Within a day or two I was released from the infirmary with a set of crutches, and an ample supply of aspirins.

It took a week or so to get my upper body built up enough to navigate the stairs and narrow halls of the class room buildings and my dorm, but I soon had it down. I was humping my way to the entrance to our dorm when I saw my dad waiting in the doorway. He had a shit-eating grin on his face as he watched me laboring away.

"Hi, dad, this is a real surprise. What brings you here?"

"Your mother, mainly. I also wanted to see what kind of idiot we had raised."

"Gee, Dad, that's a little harsh for a guy who badly injured himself in a terrible fall down the Lee Hall stairs."

"So you fell down the Lee Hall stairs huh?"

"Yeah, pretty clumsy of me, but I'm doing a lot better now that I've got the hang of these crunches."

"I have to say that I'm really relieved. Your mother had heard that you hurt yourself jumping out of a perfectly good airplane."

I was tempted to take issue with the description of "perfectly good' in relation to that damn little red piece of crap, but I decided that desecration was the better part of valor and said,

"That would be one of the dumbest stunts in the world; she probably got me mixed up with one of Benny's buddies that made his first jump week before last. He's OK now."

"That's probably what happened, I'll let her know. I feel a whole lot better about your mental state. Let's go over to the cafeteria and grab some lunch."

Author's Biography

I was born in 1939, in Dallas, Texas while my parents were on a business trip. I lived in Texas for a total of nine days while mother recovered from the trauma of my birth. Nine lousy days and I become a Texan for life. On December 11th 1941, four days after the bombing of Pearl Harbor, my Dad joined the U.S. Army in a patriotic fervor, spurred on by a generous amount of boredom with married life.

My mother went to work as a secretary in a mutations plant and I was sent to spend the war years with my maternal grandparents in Ruleville, Mississippi. If one were to design the perfect place to spend their early childhood, it would have to look a lot like Ruleville. I was barely walking when I met my across-the-street-neighbor, Billy Story, who is one month older. Billy and his brothers and sisters fill my earliest memories. He has been one of my lifelong best friends.

I started elementary school in Ruleville and can vividly remember the first day. My grandmother dressed me in a Buster Brown outfit with a lace collar and black patent leather shoes. I walked to school on that fateful day with all of the Story kids, a fact that I credit with saving my life. When the school buses unloaded their mostly barefoot and ragged charges, they took one look at me and started lining up to whip my butt. As I said, the Story boys were my salvation.

This first day of formal education held other wonders that I can still remember. I met Mrs. Slack, the first grade teacher to whom I and several hundred other kids owe a deep debt of gratitude. She gave us two things that assure one a good educational career. She taught us to read far above our grade level right out of the gate, and she instilled a sense of confidence in most of us that made sure we never felt less-than. I was fortunate to have great teachers throughout high school, but it was Mrs. Slack that paved the way for me.

The second wonder was Miss Elizabeth Stansell. There were a bunch of pretty girls in that first grade class, but Elizabeth was a pure angel. Within ten minutes of meeting her I was forever transformed. I had found my ideal of feminine beauty and grace and I would forever hold Elizabeth as the gold standard for women. She remains so to this day.

My Dad returned from the European war in 1946 was discharged as a Master Sergeant in the Army Air Corps. He went back to work for his pre-war employer and we lived in Mobile, Alabama and Monroe, Louisiana. In 1947, he re-enlisted in the newly minted U.S. Air Force. He rejoined his old commanding general and we began an odyssey of closing surplus air bases here in the U.S. and all over Central America.

I started the third grade at Lowery Air Force Base in Denver, Colorado, moved to Spokane, Washington for a winter on the Snake river that lasted about as long as the last ice age, then to the U.S. Canal Zone in Panama. If Ruleville was the ideal place to be six years old, then Panama was made for nine year olds. Later we moved to Kingston, Jamaica and finally Washington, D.C.

In mid 1950 Dad turned down the offer of a direct commission as a Captain and once again became a civilian. We moved to Cleveland, Mississippi, ten miles west of Ruleville, and I joined the fifth grade after the Christmas Holidays. I quickly fell into bad company by becoming friends with Percy Noel Funchess and Tommy Carpenter. Carpenter lived one block away from me and Noel's house was two block further on.

Once again, Cleveland was the perfect place to be for Junior and Senior High School. The Mississippi Delta was a magical place to be young, white and healthy in the 1950's. The trauma of the Civil Rights Era and the disruption of the transition from hand labor to mechanized farming were still in the foggy future and things were pretty much as they had been for the past hundred years. All of this was about to change, but we had no idea it was coming.

I played football with a group of guys in my class, Mike McCain, John Wong, T.C. Woods, G.R. Hardin and Mickey Boswell. When Company E, 155th Infantry Regiment, Mississippi National Guard returned from the Korean war a bunch of us joined to fill the ranks of re-organization, older guys like Jesse Barr and "Bear" Hazzard and younger guys like Noel and me. I was fourteen when I signed up and I enjoyed every minute for the next eight years.

In 1954 Miss Effie Glascoe who taught English in Cleveland High School, recommended me as a candidate for an annual scholarship to Philips Exeter Academy in New Hampshire. As fate would have it I was chosen to receive the honor; the only problem was I didn't want it. It was a really sweet deal; a full ride to Phillips Exeter and if successful there, a full ride to any Ivy League school that I could get into. The chance of a lifetime.

My parents were wonderful loving folks, but my mother was obsessed with her own problems and my Dad was the master of laissez faire. To say that I did not get much in the way of parental involvement would be the understatement of the century. Don't get me wrong, I liked it that way. My Dad had the attitude that he would probably be much happier if he didn't know exactly what I was doing; his only requirement was that I keep the blue lights out of his driveway.

I only mentioned the scholarship offer to them once. I chose a Sunday lunch to bring it up, knowing that mother would be anxious to get the kitchen cleaned and Dad would be itching get to his gin game. Their consensus was that I should do whatever I thought best, and mother added that it seemed a little bizarre to go to New Hampshire when there were perfectly good schools right here in Cleveland.

Freed of any parental input and left to my own devices I decided to turn the deal down. My decision was based on three primary issues: I wanted to play college football and who in hell ever heard of Dartmouth or Penn. While I assumed that New Hampshire had a National Guard organization, I knew it would be a bunch of losers compared to the 155th. Last, and in the end the deciding factor was simple, I didn't want to go to school with a bunch of damn Yankees.

Looking back over the years I have from time to time questioned my reasoning regarding Phillip Exeter. Marvin Terrell completely changed my hope of playing major college, (read, Southeastern Conference) football, my career in the National Guard came to an end after my eight-year military obligation was complete, but I never questioned the part about not wanting to spend a lot of time with a bunch of damn Yankees. Effie Glascoe never forgave me.

In the summer of 1956, between my junior and senior years, my Dad took a job in Jackson, the State Capital. Hiram Griffith's mom offered to let me stay with them for my senior year if I wanted to. Everyone assumed that moving this late in my high school career would be traumatic and that I dreaded it. Actually, I was looking forward to the change in scenery. I would have the opportunity to play Big Eight football, the biggest and best league in the state and attend a brand new high school that had knocked the top out of the national academic rankings in its inaugural year. I never looked back. I loved every minute I lived in the Mississippi Delta, but it was time for a change.

I finished high school at William B. Murrah and met some of the most important people in my life. Their stories will be the subject of another book. I completed four wonderful years at Mississippi State University and that too will be in another book.

My subsequent business career can be best described as life-long effort to avoid adult supervision. I have been a serial entrepreneur, not because I had any particular talent along those lines, but it allowed me to never have a boss. I made the decision early on that I would risk economic insecurity to achieve my personal independence. It worked out pretty well; we never went hungry and I never had to take much guff along the way.

CPSIA information can be obtained at www.ICGtesting.com
Printed in the USA
235748LV00002B/3/P

9 781849 030786